TEXAS LIGHTNING

A TEXAS BADGE MYSTERY

TEXAS LIGHTNING

A TEXAS BADGE MYSTERY

THREE TIME SPUR AWARD WINNING AUTHOR

DUSTY
RICHARDS

with VELDA BROTHERTON

 GALWAY
PRESS

an imprint of
THE OGHMA PRESS

OGHMA

CREATIVE MEDIA

Bentonville, Arkansas • Los Angeles, California
www.oghmacreative.com

Copyright © 2022 by Dusty Richards

We are a strong supporter of copyright. Copyright represents creativity, diversity, and free speech, and provides the very foundation from which culture is built. We appreciate you buying the authorized edition of this book and for complying with applicable copyright laws by not reproducing, scanning, or distributing any part of it in any form without permission. Thank you for supporting our writers and allowing us to continue publishing their books.

Library of Congress Cataloging-in-Publication Data

Names: Richards, Dusty, author | Brotherton, Velda, author
Title: Texas Lightning/Dusty Richards with Velda Brotherton | The Texas Badge #2
Description: First Edition | Bentonville: Galway, 2020
Identifiers: LCCN: 2021934735 | ISBN: 978-1-63373-596-5 (hardcover) |
ISBN: 978-1-63373-597-2 (trade paperback) | ISBN: 978-1-63373-598-9 (eBook)
BISAC: FICTION/Westerns | FICTION/Action & Adventure |
FICTION/Thrillers/Historical
LC record available at: https://lccn.loc.gov/2021934735

Galway Press trade paperback edition March, 2023

Jacket & Interior Design by Casey W. Cowan
Editing by Dennis Doty & Bob Giel

Published by Galway Press, an imprint of The Oghma Press, a subsidiary of The Oghma Book Group.

To my good buddy, Dusty Richards.
Thanks for all the years we spent together
writing, discussing and learning.

ACKNOWLEDGMENTS

A SPECIAL THANKS to Dennis Doty and Bob Giel, two superb editors, to Jeri, a daughter who keeps making my independence possible, and to Casey Cowan, who allows my writing to go on by giving me great stuff to write.

TEXAS LIGHTNING

A TEXAS BADGE MYSTERY

ONE

ROSE DREW HER COLT, STEPPED into the shadows where the dumb cowboy thought he was hiding and stuck the barrel tight against his ribs.

"You the only one?" she whispered in his ear. His stiff nod told her what she needed to know. "You got a lot to learn, you idjit. Like take off your hat, don't cough or shuffle your feet in the leaves, and for God's sake don't smoke, even if you cup a hand over the glow. I smelled it before I got off my horse."

Thought he was so smart, hunkered behind the thick shrubs. There to keep the law away from the gang down below. Make sure they were more or less safe. She'd seen him first thing when she rode up to Palo Duro Canyon and dismounted. So sure, he was invisible. Smiling, she'd kept an eye on his shadow. Way he hid, he must be new to the Jake Harper gang. If she was someone else, he'd be shot dead by now.

That was enough teaching. These were only some things that might be cut short by a bullet to his head, but not this night and not from her, being a friend of Jake's and all.

She dropped by looking for a safe place to toss out her bedroll and enjoy a decent cup of coffee. Maybe ask a few questions if they were of a mood to answer. She could be wasting her time.

Let him consider the gun in his back for a breath or two. Then, "It's me, Rose Parsons, you noisy *hombre*. A friendly visitor or you'd already be dead. Put away your gun, I've got business with Jake and his brother. Signal them I'm coming down. Do it now—if you value your ear."

He sent out a rather trembly cooing of a mourning dove that rode the evening air. He had to repeat it twice before the sharp whistle of a bob-white answered from below.

"Go on down then, and Miss Rose?"

"Don't worry, I won't tell him I rode up on you. At least not this time. Mind yourself better."

"Yep. Sure will and thanks. Uh—Miss Rose? Would you really have shot my ear off?" He sounded more resentful than grateful, but she was used to that. He'd never know the answer for sure 'cause she didn't reply.

Being a woman and a bounty hunter put two strikes against her on both the lawless and the law's side. She rode and lived in a lonely, dark world and wanted no other, not since her other world had been blown apart.

Damn, what had brought on that memory she wanted desperately to forget? With a frown she shook her head, took up Cimarron's reins, and led him down the crooked, steep trail. Its direction was marked by outlaws on the trunks of trees that clung to the steep walls into the dark bottom of the canyon. Rocks rattled from underfoot, some crashing through treetops below. No need to worry about noise now. Her childhood friend knew she was on the way.

It was good to be back in Texas after so long on the trail of that brutal killer, Rafe Malone, a man who preyed on helpless women. In her pocket was the wad of cash for turning him in, more dead than alive. Now, to take some time off from bounty hunting all over Texas and New Mexico and come home. Her strange friendship with this notorious gang might be thought dangerous by some, but she grew up in the panhandle with Jake and his brother J. T. long before the end of the war and their turning to the outlaw life. It was hands off on both sides when they were together.

The Harper Gang was mostly ex-Confederate soldiers and a few strays they'd picked up of the like persuasion. All were trying to make up for what Texas had lost during that vicious war between the states. Like the James Gang back in Missouri and Arkansas, most of their take stolen from bankers and carpetbaggers went to the people too poor to have food or a roof over their heads.

She'd just take time to say hello and see if they knew anything about the rumor she'd heard on her way, that a fire starter was running around in the panhandle burning up ranch houses when the families were inside. Good to know what made people do what they did, that's for sure. Hard to figure this one out, though. It looked like she wouldn't have much time off with a reward of two thousand dollars on his head.

Some bounty hunters killed their prey. Chopped off their head, put it in a gunny sack and carried it to the nearest ranger or sheriff's office for pay. Most wanted posters said dead or alive. She wasn't fond of the chopped off head method, but there were times when she might do just that—and this was one of them.

Tomorrow she'd be on her way after the bastard. Maybe visit a while with Mama before moving on in pursuit of this fire devil whose wanted poster she'd picked up the day before. Only a crude drawing that gave her no idea what he looked like. Jake might know something.

Home place was still thirty miles away. But on the flat country of Texas the long-legged bay could make it in a day without breathing too hard.

Visiting with Jake would ease her sore heart. As a bounty hunter she often saw terrible things, like the unfortunate women cut to pieces by Rafe Malone. She could try to wash the memories out of her mind by visiting with friends and family before moving on. There was no shortage of the worst sinners, and in her business, she couldn't avoid them.

In the rugged bottom of the canyon, she walked her mount toward the gang's hideout, the crumbling remains of an old dwelling.

Jake emerged from a gaping door, backlit by firelight, and recognized her. "Well, I'm damned, girl. I was beginning to think you'd gone the way of the dodo."

A night breeze kissed her cheek, and she imagined the one who once touched his lips there. Lost now. She managed soft laughter. "You read too much, Jake. How are you, anyway?"

"Tolerable, child, just plain tolerable. Still, plenty of banks to rob, then there's always the trains if they give out."

"Leave that hoss there with Rocky and come on over by the fire. J. T. will be pleased to see you."

She doubted that, since Jake's brother judged her as being on the same side of the fence as lawmen. Yet he wouldn't have fisticuffs with his brother over the friendship.

J. T. rose but withheld his hand "Good to see you, Rose."

Jake turned, a steaming tin cup in his hand. "Have some coffee and sit a spell. Where you on your way to now?"

"Around Carlton. Some trouble brewing, I can take a hand in." The crackle from her pocket was the folded wanted poster for the bastard she pursued. He'd been working around the fairly new settlement about a day's ride from Amarillo. She wouldn't tell Jake that in front of these men. They didn't need to know too much about the Texas Rose lest one of them get overly hungry for the bucks offered on her own wanted poster, or God forbid, the evil doer himself was part of this gang.

Instead of explaining further, she sipped coffee and exchanged rides and troubles on the trail with them. Later in private, when the gang members snored except for the rim-top guard, she felt Jake out about the fire starter, but saw right away he either knew nothing or had decided not to talk. A sign she needed to keep the remainder to herself. That, so far, Rangers and Marshals had been unable to catch up to him. The sheriff of Legend County had ridden up on him and got himself killed for his troubles leaving the town of Carlton in dire straits for law.

Dell Hoffman, sheriff of Saddler County, a bit northwest of there was taking care of the law for both 'til someone could be appointed. Hoffman was a tough, experienced man with plenty of big arrests under his belt. He was up to the job, but he needed assistance.

As a bounty hunter she could take some of the lawbreakers off his table, if only he allowed her presence. Her business was nobody's but her own. The destructive fires around Carlton and the death of the sheriff were a perfect reason for a bounty hunter to step in but talking about it could get her killed. Jake knew not to butt in either. After all, he had his own secrets to keep.

They talked a while before he offered her a place to lay her head nearby, and she took it. She'd stop and see Mama who lived on the Legend/Saddler County line, on her way. It was a long ride to Legend County and the burnt ranches around Carlton so she'd take her fellowship where she could get it. While she dragged her saddle off Cimarron, J. T. approached on padded feet.

"Rosie, do you suppose I could talk to you a minute?"

She continued to remove the saddlebag and lay out her blanket. "Sure, J. T. What is it?" Though she figured she knew, she waited for him to bring it up.

"It's this way. You coming around when we're hid out could bring us nothing but trouble."

Absolutely right, the same old complaint, no matter where she saw him. He wanted it to be ignoring each other, like people paid any attention.

She gestured around them. "Sort of nobody out here but us chickens, as they say. These men already know about our friendship since we were kids. What's the problem? You must know I'm never followed."

"Jest trying to tell you the dangers is all." He carried a chip on his shoulder, no doubt. In a way, she couldn't blame him, yet it was her who should dislike him. He'd got the man she loved killed back in the war. He knew she knew it, and like some men, put up a wall fueled by guilt. Not something she could do anything about.

She placed her saddle at the head of the blanket and sat down. "Why don't you go tell Jake about it, J.T. Maybe he'll do something. I have to get some sleep. I'll be gone in the morning, so nothing to worry about."

Sunrise awakened the morning with swirls of taffy-like pink and gold clouds. Rose roused early and finished the dregs of the previous night's coffee. Like most spring days on the plains of northern Texas, it would be windy, dry and beautiful. True to her word, Rose rode out with the dawn, not bothering to awaken anyone.

Cookie glanced up from the chuck-wagon and grinned when she grabbed a biscuit left from the day before. "You come see us again, Miss Rosie. It's good to hear and see a purty woman."

She swallowed. "I'll try. You keep making good beans and taters."

"I will, ma'am. You ride easy now."

She flipped the brim of her black Stetson with three fingers. "You do the same, Cookie."

Leading her horse from the deep canyon onto the flat Texas plains, she raised her face to the brisk wind and warming sun, scanned her sur-roundings as if adjusting her latigo, mounted and pointed the horse toward Legend County and her next job.

That same sun hung on the curved rim of the earth when the small town of Thomas City spread out before her. She was bone tired and ready for a bath, and this looked like the right proper place to have one, and maybe a juicy fat-rimmed steak. She could be at Mama's before dark, washed and fed. Mama lived in a well-hidden deep cut above the Red River just after it curved and headed southeast. Trees surrounded the small cabin. Mama didn't like company, barely tolerated Rose's visits. But she was Rose's only family, her brother, Charles, having been killed in the war. Mama died in her heart and soul then, and Rose knew how that felt.

The sign for Thomas City announced a population of 1,568 which made it a decent sized settlement for the wildness of the Texas panhan-dle. She reined in at a hitching rail in front of the public bathing house. Swinging off, she palmed the Colt and tucked it into her saddlebag. Sheriff

Dell Hoffman was a stickler for armed visitors, and she'd rather not call attention to herself by leaving it. She'd be gone before it made a difference.

SHERIFF HOFFMAN DONNED HIS STETSON and stepped out onto

the boardwalk into the slanted rays of an evening sun. Who in thunder was that down the street just getting off her horse? Had to be Rosie Parsons, the only woman bounty hunter he knew of. Her sun-streaked hair was kept under control by a black Stetson. In her boots she was six feet tall and wore britches and the brightest silken shirts he'd ever seen. Only woman he knew who rode clothespin on a huge red Andalusian bay—the finest horse in the panhandle, so far as he was concerned.

Hadn't seen her in a while. He'd bet she was on the trail of some mean outlaw. She preferred to chase down the biggest, orneriest men left walking rather than finding herself a good husband. Why that was, he had no notion. Maybe she wouldn't be in town long. Could be going home to see her Ma, though, who lived over near the Legend County line.

Off down the street someone shouted, someone else shot off a gun. Enough to stop his wondering about seeing Rosie and head toward the hubbub. As his town prospered, keeping the peace took more and more of his time. Who in thunder had managed to sneak in with his sidearm?

The two men had chased each other around the corner and Dell held back there, gun drawn, to peer around and gauge what was up. They faced each other, one waving a gun around, the other unarmed, and both too drunk to stand without staggering around. Probably couldn't see each other. That made the drawn gun more dangerous.

Dell crept into the center of the street 'til he was right behind the armed cowboy and poked him fast before backing away.

"Feel that, Pense?" Dell spat in the dust.

Frozen, the fella grunted, "Uh-huh."

"Put yours down, now, 'fore I clock you one."

The other man, a stranger to Dell, held both hands away from his body, but he swayed from side to side. "Don't let him shoot me, sheriff."

"He ain't gonna shoot you. Stay put, mister."

Pense changed his mind and pulled the trigger in the instant Dell eyed the second man. His aim was off so much his shot sprayed dust from the middle of the road. He whirled, putting Dell in his sights.

Danged fast for a drunk. Dell was faster, dropping to one knee, but before he could shoot back someone else fired from where the street teed. Pense dropped like a poleaxed beef and Dell swung toward the sharp sound. Rosie stood in the middle of the road a good sixty or seventy feet from the men, a smoking Colt in one hand.

"Dang me, gal. Don't you know that we don't allow weapons in the town limits?"

"Sorry, Sheriff. I just plain forgot, what with that man pointing one at you."

Pense sat feet splayed, holding his shoulder and glaring at her. "You didn't have to shoot me, did you?"

Dell pulled the wounded man to his feet, sweeping his weapon up as he did. "You there, you get to take him over to Doc, right above the General Mercantile. Make sure he pays." He pointed at the stranger.

The fella's bearded face screwed up, but he stopped swaying. The gunplay must've sobered him up. "Me? I didn't shoot him."

"Don't matter, now git 'fore I put you in a cell instead. And you stay with him 'til he rides out, you hear?"

The man stared for a moment, gestured toward Rose. "What about her? She's got a gun, too."

"True, and we sure wouldn't want her to start shooting again, would we? Now go on, the two of you."

A crowd had gathered, mostly ladies in town shopping, but a few men on horseback slowed to take a good look at Rosie, holding a smoking six shooter. He didn't much blame them, either. While he kept an eye on the two drunks, she put her gun away and approached, laughing.

"Good way to end a day, huh sheriff?" Her shadow crawled across the dusty road beside him.

Half-grinning, he held out a hand. She grasped it and shook hard as a man. A gust of wind raised dust between them, and the crowd milled about as if expecting more of a show between the tall woman and their sheriff. When it appeared the action was over, they went on their way.

"What you doing out this way?" He let go her hand and tucked the extra gun into his belt.

"You want mine, too?"

"Turn it in to the office, they'll give you a chit for it. You didn't say what brings you here. Come to see your mama?"

"That and other business. You got yourself a real renegade running the plains hereabouts. Thought you could use some help catching him." She grinned.

"You mean the arsonist. Nice of you to offer. I got me some extra deputies nowadays, though."

She nodded, and when he turned to leave the street, she followed. "Guess you'll need them, what with the sheriff over in Legend County taking a bullet. I was sorry to hear that. Gus Talken was a good man. An honest man. Getting harder and harder to find those."

Taking the steps onto the boardwalk, she turned to go in the opposite direction. "I just stopped to take a bath. I'll move on when I'm done, but I'll take my gun into your office anyway. Don't ache to break any laws, especially in your town. I been hearing about your arrests down in El Paso and saving those children. Good for you, Dell. I'll be around if you decide I can be of help in your search for this heathen killer."

He nodded, held out his hand. "I'll just leave it at the office with Brand. Save you going down there. Going home for a spell?"

"Thought I would." She handed him the Colt with no objection.

For a minute there, he thought she wasn't going to hand it over, and he took it with relief. Coming to a showdown with Rosie didn't appeal to him at all. He held it down at his side. "Tell your Ma I said hello."

"Will do. Shall I bring back her reply?"

"Naw, don't bother. I kind of have an idea what it'd be."

They shared a laugh, bid each other good evening and walked in opposite directions down the dirt road. The setting sun laid a golden path down the center of town. The boardwalks emptied of traffic and only one or two wagons remained.

Setting off toward the office, he couldn't help but ponder a gal like Rosie hunting killers. Now, here she was back in Texas after the fire starter. How a woman could spend her days running down the worst of the worst, often breaking the law herself, was a tough one to figure out. You'd think she'd be home having babies with the man she loved. But he'd heard tales too harsh to ponder about her past and what turned her into a bounty hunter in one of the toughest states in the Union. Odd though, he admired the woman and her fortitude.

After leaving her Colt at the office, he walked each side of the street checking to make sure all the stores were safely locked up. It was a job he wouldn't have had a year ago, but then McIlroy bought the bank, covered all the loses, and businesses reopened their doors. Even some new ones moved in.

Now, they had a bank, a blacksmith and a farrier, a saddlery, a barber, and a bathhouse—just all manner of things. The old mercantile was all new and expanded, another church had come to town to join the Methodist one, a new schoolteacher was hired, and he'd heard that some fancy woman from Amarillo was opening a house of entertainment next to the saloon. There would be the most trouble, but overall, he was proud of Thomas City.

A while later he backed out the door of the jail and pulled it shut on the constant babble of Brand, his night deputy. Now that the town was prosperous again, Dell had hired a couple more deputies besides Fred Hanks. With a bit of prosperity always came an increase in law breakers. Everything from petty thefts to grand larceny and murder. Sometimes you had to pay heavily when you got what we wished for, and he had wished the town would stagger back to its feet after the big bank robbery a while back.

He hoped he hadn't made a mistake choosing Brand. He liked younger men because they hadn't been molded into someone else's idea of a lawman yet. Not much more than a kid, he probably talked to himself most of the night 'cause he didn't know when to shut up. It might be funny if he snuck up on him and throw'd the door open sometime to catch him preaching, but he didn't see the point. Long as the boy did his job, he could turn him into a proper deputy.

Lord knows there was plenty of work until Legend County appointed a new sheriff. Men weren't anxious to step into the boots of a murdered sheriff, and you couldn't blame them. Meanwhile he had some work cut out for himself.

Someone had to put a stop to the fire starter's dreadful work. Burning folks up while they slept in their homes had to be the worst thing one could imagine. That was who Rosie referred to earlier, calling him a bastard. Harsh words for a pretty lady. If she saw fit to go after him, she could get herself killed.

Out on the boardwalk, he tilted his head back and slid the Stetson on. Scuffing dust from the planks, he picked up his pace and rounded the corner toward his house. His wife Guinn's cooking filled the air with a delicious aroma long before he opened the door, stomped the dirt off his boot, and hollered out to her.

The most beautiful woman in the world stepped from the kitchen. Curls escaping her red hair drawn away from cheeks flushed with cooking a supper that smelled wonderful.

"I'm right here, cowboy. No need to holler like you're fetching your cattle." She smiled to show she was joking and held out her arms.

Boy did he look forward to a few hours hugged close to that body. Her touch had a way of driving off the worries of keeping his town safe from the evil deeds of others.

"Come on in here. Don't let the flies turn around and follow you."

He grinned, stepped in and let the door shut behind him before embracing her. She was one heck of a woman who filled his heart and soul with wonderment that he'd ever been lucky enough to find her. He still blessed the day he'd met her. He kissed the moist flesh beneath her ear, the fragrance of bread in his nostrils.

"Sit, I'll pour you lemonade." He did and she laid a hand on the back of his neck. Her blue eyes were cloudy with worry. "Heard a shot in town today. Everything okay?"

"Oh, sure. Couple of damn drunks, that's all. One just managed to bring in his gun."

"Mmm. Anyone hurt?"

"Rose Parsons shot one of them. Not bad."

"You're kidding. How'd *she* get into town armed? You surely didn't give her a pass, pretty as she is."

"Of course not, it was kind of an all-at-once-happening." He drank half the glass of tart lemonade. "Mmm, good and that bread smells good too."

She grabbed a potholder and opened the oven. Removing two loaves of bread, she brought one to the table. "You might want to wash up. Supper's almost ready."

They ate on the back verandah away from the heat of the cook stove, discussing the day's happenings and exchanging tales from earlier memories. It was a long time before they rose and went in the house to bed. Seemed to Dell they spent a lot of time sharing stories out of their pasts.

Guinn was the first woman he'd ever felt this comfortable with. Though it wasn't something folks supported much, he was real happy she'd finally got her divorce so they could marry. He'd hated sneaking around with a married woman after her husband took off. It wasn't seemly, and he feared too much talk about her around town, especially when Teddy was born a few months after their legal wedding. But everyone congratulated them and went on about their business.

He tried not to think of the beautiful, curly-haired little boy. It was so painful to remember him fighting whooping cough with so much pain. When he succumbed while Guinn held him in her arms, he thought she might never recover. He almost hadn't himself.

He pushed away memories of the dreadful dark time of their life and smiled at his lovely wife. Life was how it was, and all one could do was push on to the next surprise it had to offer. Meanwhile, he helped with the dishes, then followed Guinn upstairs to the bedroom where they would share the love both felt so fortunate to have.

TWO

ROSE MEANT TO GET TO Mama's earlier, but by the time she arrived, Cimarron picked his way in dusky shadows up the long, hidden path from the river. Halfway there a peculiar smell in the air halted her—like smoke and something worse. Tiny flames flickered, visible through the thick brush. Fire?

"Whoa, boy." Heart racing, she jerked at the reins to check the bay's nervous dancing. Nostrils flaring, ears laid back, he crow-hopped sideways. Tightening the bridle to keep him from rearing, she stroked the tight muscles of his neck. "Easy there. Take it easy, boy."

But the horse was having none of it. His natural fear of fire took over and he hopped backward and tossed his head.

Leaning forward over his neck to stop the movement, her own heart thundered 'til she could barely catch her breath. "Mama. Mama!" Screaming she let go the hold on Cimarron, swung off and raced the remaining feet to the clearing where Mama's cabin lay in ruins. Against patterns of silvery sky, smoking, flickering timbers were heaped around what had once been her home, Mama's home since leaving Dottie Lou's in Fort Smith.

"Mama, oh God, no." Her choking words broke the evening silence.

She cried her name, over and over. What if she never heard her or saw her again? Time to control herself and learn what had happened. Handle it.

Mama. Where was Mama?

Maybe she was outside. Maybe she was safe. But, if so, where? In the burnt timbers lumps that were the stove, the bedstead, a tin kitchen cabinet and thicker hunks of lumber marked all that was left. Calling her name, checking the outhouse, nothing fetched Mama.

Poor Mama, in there somewhere. Unable to escape. Flames eating at her body. She couldn't imagine the terror, the pain, the clawing for breath and the final giving in. How long would the minutes be while her body was consumed by fire? In her grief, she gasped for air herself.

Darkness closed in around her where she slumped beside the ruins of the small cabin. There Mama had spent her last horrific moments of life. A dumb acceptance of what she had lost left Rose unable to speak or think. Tears poured down her cheeks. How long she huddled there she didn't know. It might have been forever.

Coming back to reality she screamed for Mama, tried to tear through the jumble, find her, drag her from the ruins, but it was still too hot. The soles of her boots were hot, sparks flamed at the hem of her britches and she kicked her way free. She had to stumble out. There was nothing more she could do 'til it cooled off and daylight broke. If Mama had escaped and was hiding nearby, she would've heard her by now and come out. She could only lay dead. Burned up in the wreckage.

In her nostrils the stench of kerosene and something else like flesh cooking she refused to think about. Her mind settled then on the other smell. Kerosene. A fire deliberately set. If she had been here sooner, she wouldn't have missed the bastard who did this.

The fire starter? Could it be? But why Mama? She'd never done anything to anyone. Maybe her younger life was considered sinning, but for the past years, she'd lived up here growing her flowers and some vegetables, rocking on the porch and singing in her clear perfect voice. How dare someone do this? She'd find the son-of-a-bitch and put him in his grave, cut off his head and carry it to the Rangers as proof for her reward.

Shedding tears that refused to stop she moved away from the coals and found the nervous Cimarron hiding in the brush away from the smoking pyre. Deep in the woods where she could no longer smell the smoke, she dragged off the saddle, bags and bedroll, and made camp for the night. Come morning she'd find his trail and follow him to the gates of hell if necessary. But she would find him and give him his due, and then some.

Tonight, she'd spend here near Mama, their last night together. Before she could settle for the night, the drum of horses' hooves roused her from the dark grief of her loss. She came to her feet, Colt gripped in one hand. Someone calling her name, Mama's name.

"Here, I'm here." She waved her hand and hurried toward the clearing where several men waited on horseback.

One doffed his hat. "Rosie, it's Dell. Dell Hoffman. Your neighbor saw the flames, but couldn't get in right away. He was shoeing his horse. Anyone hurt here? Could we help? These here are deputies from Carlton, your place being on the county line."

"Can't find my Mama." She was hoarse and pointed. "She's in there somewhere… I couldn't … I was too late to save her."

"Miss Rosie, with your permission we'll look around. She may have gotten out, could be hiding and fell asleep."

The three men rode past, hats doffed in silence, and began to search in an ever-widening circle calling, "Miz Parsons, you here?" over and over. There was no reply. The woods remained still, as if in respect to the woman's passing. Even the frogs over on Jeeter Pond hushed in reverence.

Jaw set tight, Rose waited in one spot 'til the horsemen came back. They wouldn't find anyone. Mama's body lay in there beneath what was left of the brass bedstead. Her laudanum-laced sleep hopefully giving her a merciful death.

Fists clenched against her thighs, Rosie murmured an oath. The man who did this would have no painless death, she would see to that. Whether the wanted poster read dead or alive. She would haul him in headless and belly down on a horse. "Sheriff?"

"Yes'm, Miss Rosie? Guinn says to bring you home with me. She's making a bed in the attic room. Jest 'til your tears turn to rage."

"I appreciate it, Sheriff. But they already have done that. I hope you understand what I have to do?"

"Yes'm, and my duty is clear, too. I pray we don't run across each other in the process."

"This man has fired half a dozen ranches now all over the panhandle. Killed twice that many people. It don't appear he's going to stop anytime soon. How come he chose Mama, I'll never know. He'll keep on 'less one of us stops him. Law's out after him from several counties. I've seen the wanteds."

"I reckon you're right, Miss Rose. I'm truly sorry, but I 'spect we'll find Miz Parsons' body once this cools down. You coming back to town with me?"

Rose stared at the ground for a minute. "I think I'd best stay here overnight. I'll be leaving out early, and I wouldn't want to disturb you."

"You won't disturb me nor my wife. We'll be getting me ready to ride out in search of this heathen killer. I do wish you'd remain at our home with Guinn."

She squinted up. "You know I can't do that."

"What if I said I'd have to arrest you?"

"I'd say you might try, Sheriff." She spat the final word at him, turned and stomped back into the woods where she'd earlier made her sleeping camp.

Danged old fool wasn't about to put a stop to her searching for this evil man. Without her, he might never catch him on his own. Course, being a man, he'd never admit that, not even in silence to himself. If she didn't respect the sheriff, she'd just shoot him to lay him up a while and finish this herself, the right way. With a bullet to the gut. She'd watch this killer suffer a long, long time before she claimed her reward.

With sadly murmured farewells, the riders rode off, the clopping of their horse's hooves leaving behind a silence so deep and dark Rose ached to flee this place of death. But there were tracks to follow only in daylight. She would visit with Mama one last time. She never went to sleep that night, just lay there conversing with Mama, who she'd never really got along with that well. But that didn't matter. They were family and she loved her. Besides, you didn't turn your back on family, no matter what they did to you.

Come pre-dawn with birdsong and a sky the color of polished steel, she untied the hobble from Cimarron's front legs, saddled up, and walked ahead of him to begin her search for tracks leading away from all those cut in the ground by the sheriff and his deputies the night before. It took a while to separate them out, but she finally rode away from Mama's final resting place and followed the set of tracks that left out from all the others.

On her knees, running fingers over the casting in the dirt, she paused. Looked closer. There, through one side of the shoe was a faint crack—almost like a lightning strike. Made it easy to follow. The bastard was headed southwest across the great plains toward the Guadalupe Mountains.

He wasn't going to make it.

GUINN LEANED AGAINST THE BEDROOM doorway, arms crossed

under her breasts. "I don't understand why Rose didn't come here. We need to find her Mama's bones and bury them. Have a funeral so she can grieve properly. She needs to be here."

"Now, Guinn, we both know Rose. Have since she was a stubborn child. Who knows what fuels her fire? All we know is she sure has one and it burns furious inside her." He dug deeper on the chifforobe floor. "Where's my spare ground cover?"

She pushed away from the wall, moved toward the back porch and came back carrying the oilcloth folded neatly. "Why an extra one?"

"This won't be a two or three-day affair. That woman will chase that bastard clear into the mountains. So will we, and up there we'll need protection. You know how the storms get up there in late winter."

Guinn laid a gentle hand on his arm. "What makes you think she'll go into the mountains?"

Grim-lipped, he patted her hand. "Or wherever this killer leads her. I hate to say it, but I hope he does go into the mountains rather than staying out here setting fires. Rosie's a good tracker, so I'll stay on her trail wherever she goes. We have to be prepared, no matter what. You be all right here? We can get a girl from town to stay with you. I don't like you being alone with men like this one running around out there. You know, things didn't used to be so damned dangerous, but more and more folk flowing into Texas means the bad ones will come with them. 'Fore long, I'll probably need more deputies just to protect Thomas City."

"Don't be silly, Dell. I'll be fine. What could a girl do for me I can't do myself? I'm a pretty good shot." She turned and went back into the kitchen where she was cooking corn fritters and biscuits for him to carry along with beef jerky and coffee.

Not willing to give up yet, Dell went to the doorway. "Well, she could keep you company so you could compare your prowess with a gun, I reckon."

When she laughed, he couldn't help joining her. Thus, their brief disagreements went, one of the main reasons he loved her so much. She got her way using a soft voice and well-chosen words and never shouted.

She returned while he stuffed his saddlebags with clothing and socks to keep him warm on those cold nights. She slipped her arms around his waist from behind. "I love you, Dell Hoffman. You be careful out there and don't stay gone too long. I might just forget you for a younger man."

Again, they laughed together.

He dropped the bags on the floor, turned and took her in his arms, rubbing one hand up under her blouse. "How could I stay away from you for very long? Are the fritters and biscuits done?"

She touched her cheek to his. "Yes."

He found the buttons on her blouse and fumbled the first one open. "Good. Very good."

In the early morning light outside the jailhouse, while much of the town still slept, old Fred Hanks kicked at the dirt while Dell tied down his bedroll.

"I don't think it's a good idea for you to go alone, Sheriff. Why'd you hire Brand for if it ain't so I can go on manhunts with you?"

"Why'd I hire him? To stay here and help you keep the town safe while I'm gone. Now don't be childish. You make sure everyone is safe and locked up every night and no one gets in town with a gun on their hip. Get help from Marshal Burns or deputize Dutch. He's always anxious to lend a hand."

"What we need is more of us, what with the town growing like it is. You ought to do something about that."

"Just as soon as I get back. We got more already. Now move back so I can get on my way." Dell swung into the saddle and reined away from the complaining deputy. The pack animal he'd borrowed from Cletus Jones was a small, stout jack, a bit stubborn but strong as a bull.

"So, when you reckon you'll be back?

"Long as it takes." He carried enough supplies to stay out a week or more, but he hoped it didn't take that long to run down this arsonist. With one last harsh stare at Hanks, he leaned forward. "Check on my wife once in a while, would you? See you soon."

He heeled his mount gently, all he ever took, and rode straight down the middle of the road through town, Curly raising enough dust to earn him a tongue-lashing from old Mrs. Lowry in the Mercantile if she'd been awake to see it. Little Jack trotted along behind loaded with enough to keep him fed, clothed and dry for at least a week. Somewhere out there ahead of him the Rose of Texas followed her nose. He hoped he didn't have to tangle with her. What one thought was right didn't always suit the other, and she seldom followed the rules.

He'd known Rose long enough to know that when she got hold of something she wouldn't let go. Let her get her teeth in something, and she'd rag it to death before turning loose. He might step back and let her get this man if he wasn't so dangerous. Besides, he was the law enforcement around here. She'd worked for her mama in Ft. Smith for a while, and he understood she did very well. But it wasn't exciting enough for her. After disappearing for several years, she turned up back in the panhandle where she'd been raised. This time making a living chasing known outlaws.

Many a sheriff jailed bounty hunters when they could, but he was loath to do that to the only female one in four counties or more. Besides, she weeded out the hardest to catch. Had a nose like a bloodhound for where they'd run to and was tough enough to catch them.

Heading southwest in pursuit of Rose made sense for a lot of reasons, the first being that many of the Fort Smith Marshals rode Indian Territory. Combined with the Texas Rangers, they kept a tight rein to the east. If this guy got busy over there, they'd take him out quick as could be. Old Judge Parker would be delighted to hang him faster than you could bat an eye.

No, the fire starter would keep working the panhandle of Texas, until he wiped out all the ranchers he had a taste for. Knowing why he held his grudge would help a lot, but, as of yet, Dell had no idea. Maybe he was simply burning out people at random rather than for a reason. Someone might catch him at it, but he couldn't count on it. Once in a while, Dell could count on a tough old settler to take out a law breaker before he could get to him.

He would cover Saddler County first, 'cause that was his territory. But seeing as how Legend County was temporarily without a sheriff, he had a duty to help out over there 'til a new one was appointed—which hopefully would be any day now. The vast countryside of the Texas panhandle took plenty of lawmen, but some counties were lucky to have more than one. Thing was, he had his to cover first, but on the other hand, this devil had struck in his so he might follow him to the ends of the earth to make him pay.

Rangers would lend a hand, but they too were scarce in some areas. The highest crime spots earned the most Ranger coverage, so the panhandle made do with town marshals like Fred Hanks.

A thin spiral of smoke rose from the Parson place as he crossed from Saddler into Legend County. He wondered if they'd found Miz Dottie's body yet. If he wanted, he could borrow one of the deputies from Carlton a few miles on up the road. It might be a good idea to have help with capturing this yahoo. The problem with it was the fact that Legend County's sheriff had been killed a while back, and the town had been short on law ever since. Miz Dottie lived right near to the county line, so he could be said to be legal in hunting down those outlaws even outside of his jurisdiction.

He didn't get the chance to ride on past, though. Two cowboys, hell-bent-for-leather, approached from the direction of the burnt cabin. Not many out-of-towners knew of the place, seeing as how Miz Dottie liked her privacy and often ran folks off, even when she knew them. So, Dell held up and went to meet them.

"What the thunder's going on?" Curly skittered sideways and kicked up dust, blocking their way. "Sheriff Dell Hoffman. Just hold up a minute."

One of the men attempted to go around, but Dell drew down on him. "I said just hold up there. Don't make me repeat myself. Let's get this matter settled. I asked what's going on. All you gotta do is answer."

"We didn't have nothing to do with that fire, Sheriff. Honest to God."

"What you doing up there, then?"

"Looking for Miss Rosie. We didn't know this happened."

"How do you know Rosie?"

The two men studied each other as if trying to decide who could or should answer the question. Then the youngest, a long-haired kid trying to grow a bush over his lip with little success, shrugged. "She come to visit yesterday asking questions, and we sort of heard some answers."

Dell scratched his chin. Should he try to learn what they knew, send them on their way, or take them in in the hopes he could make them talk?

"When did you see Rose last? Did you know her Mama burned up in that fire?"

The older one looked upset, but hard to tell why. "Aw, we're sorry to hear that. She was on her way to visit her Mama when she dropped by our—uh—place."

The two men stared at the ground.

"This have anything to do with the fires here in Legend county?"

"No, shoot no, but if you see Rose tell her Dockery is looking for her. Could you do that?"

"Dockery, huh? Where you from?"

"Over Glennon way. We'll see her soon. Good day, sir." Dockery kept an eye on Dell while back walking his shaggy roan and kicking him in the ribs. The young one rode slowly along beside him.

Dell watched them go without a word.

RATHER THAN RIDE ON INTO Carlton looking for a room, he drew
up outside of town under a small grove of cottonwoods. Tying the two animals to a line, he gathered up plenty of wind-broke limbs to keep a fire going into the night and, after feeding the animals, settled down to supper and an early night.

Laying on his back, staring up at the star-strewn sky, gave him time to ponder things. For whatever reason, the unusual meeting with the two cowboys didn't sit right in his craw, though he was finally able to recall where he'd met Dockery before. He'd been with a bunch come through Thomas City last fall. They were a noisy, rowdy bunch, but finally gave up their weapons and spent a few hours in the saloon before moving on. Nothing memorable, but he'd always had a feeling about them. Like he knew them from somewhere important. He'd remember them both now, though. Better believe he would.

The real question was if they had anything to do with this runaway fire starter, and if so, how?

He sighed. The thought made him realize just how little he actually had to go on here. There was no physical evidence, and no apparent motive. He'd told Guinn he'd be following Rosie. She was pretty good at catching owl-hoots no one else could find. But as he thought about it more, other potential angles of investigation began to occur to him. He fell asleep with some ideas stewing in his brain, least of which was to run Rose down and follow her around.

IN CARLTON THE NEXT MORNING, Dell tied his animals outside the

sheriff's office and went in on the chance someone might have been appointed to take Sheriff Moon's place. He could exchange information and see where they stood in running down the fire starter.

A red-headed kid with a skinny neck and a prominent Adam's apple sat behind the sheriff's desk, a pair of well-worn boots propped there. They hit the wood floor with a hard thunk when the kid spotted him. Probably spied his badge pinned on his jacket pocket.

"Afternoon, son. Your father here?" Dell smiled inwardly at the insult. He couldn't help himself. A man who finds no humor in a tough job isn't long for keeping it.

"You ain't my pa. But I can get him for you, and he'll clean your plow."

So much for that approach. "Watch your tongue, boy. I have jurisdiction to drag you off to jail. I want to know who's in charge here, and I want to talk to him. Now." He punched the desktop hard enough to rattle a glass bowl with a cigar butt in it and glared at the kid.

Probably time he watched his temper. What was going on in his county had sure set him on edge. The kid might just come out of that room with someone who could clean his plow. Then where would he be?

The kid's coppery eyes flared, but he slid from behind the desk and disappeared through a door along the back wall. He soon returned with a man who could not deny fathering the kid.

Dell was pleased to see that the half-pint couldn't come near cleaning his plow. "Yeah, how can I help you?"

Had a mouth on him, too. "Sheriff Dell Hoffman, from over in Saddler County. You would be?" He waited patiently while the freckle-faced man considered his question.

"Deputy Sheriff Dirks. What do you need, mister?"

Enough of this game. "I'm pursuing a fire starter who's burning homes and people in them. Any of that going on in Legend County?"

"I don't think that's any of your business, Sheriff." "You happen to know of Miz Dottie Lou's place burning last night?"

"Oh, her? Figure she fell asleep and left a candle burning. Prob'ly set the curtains on fire. Crazy old woman. Besides, technically, it's a bit on the Legend County line and we're short on men here."

Determined to teach the fella some manners without slugging him in the mouth, which, when you thought of it, wasn't exactly the way to teach anything but more violence, Dell ground his teeth over his next words. "Well, if I were you, I'd get me some men, 'cause that crazy coot is headed this way. And he don't care who he kills. I—"

Dell stopped. A thought had suddenly occurred to him, and an unpleasant one at that. "Tell me, did you ride in the posse that burned out Amos Horner and his family a few weeks ago?"

Horner was a convicted killer who'd manage to escape from the authorities out Amarillo way. For whatever reason—he wasn't exactly the sharpest tool in the box—he'd made his way back to the homeplace on the county line not far from Miz Dottie's. He'd been spotted almost immediately, and a posse had been formed to bring him in. That's when things had taken a turn. Cornering him in his house with his wife and children, the impatient posse leaders opted not to wait for him to surrender, choosing instead to burn him out. Horner and his eldest son escaped, but his wife and young daughter did not.

The incident had stirred up all sorts of trouble in both counties. Shock and anger on one side over the senseless killing of an innocent woman and little girl. Righteous indignation on the other since Horner was an escaped killer and the posse had felt they were justified in their actions.

Dell himself felt some measure of personal guilt for the outcome, as well. He'd been off in San Angelo testifying in court on another case. In his absence, a couple of hotheaded ranchers from the outskirts of Saddler County had organized the pursuit without consulting Dell's deputies. Had he been here... had he been leading the posse like he should have, none of it would have happened.

The arrogant little cuss shook his head. "Nah. Like I said, we're short of men. I couldn't be spared. I do know some who did, though."

"Well, you might ride out and warn them—or send someone if you're too busy." Dell deliberately stared around the room to make his point.

"I'll think about it."

"And you haven't heard anything about this from anyone, or seen someone looking crazy enough to be doing such a thing?"

"Not that I know of."

Dell sighed. How in hell had this little weasel ever become a deputy? I'd like to take a look at your wanteds, too, if you don't mind. Looking for a particular face, name of Dockery."

"Be my guest." The ugly-mouthed man pointed to the far wall where a thick sheaf of wanted posters were tacked. "Just put 'em back up when you're finished."

He really didn't have the time for this, but that fella's face—the one who claimed to know Rose—bothered him. He touched the brim of his hat, smiled and said in a kind voice, "Thank you so much for your hospitality."

The man just stared at him. If one of his deputies treated anyone this way, Dell would have thrown him out on his ass in a heartbeat.

He hurriedly paged through the posters but saw no reference to a Dockery. He shrugged, tacked them precisely back on the wall and caught the deputy opening the door to the cells.

"Can you tell me with this? Has a new man been appointed to take Sheriff Moon's place? We're gonna need a posse to get after this devil and shut him down 'fore he kills more folks. I could use some deputies or a ranger to help out."

"We ain't got no lawmen to spare, as you might have heard about the shootout here. And I ain't seen no rangers, neither."

Dell stared at the man for a moment. What happened to people that they got so sour-mouthed? He reconsidered the violent way of teaching a lesson, instead touched the brim of his hat again. "Well, thanks again for your hospitality. You have you a fine day, if you can."

He turned and left without waiting for an answer.

UNLIKE THOMAS CITY, DELL HAD heard that Carlton had it's own small newspaper. Leaving Curly and his companion tied up outside the jail, he found the office a block further down down Main Street. A sign on the door read, *AT THE CAFÉ TIL 9.* Shaking his head, he retraced his steps, passing the jail again and crossing the street to the bank. Right next door stood the Early Sun Café, an outfit he'd visited many times before.

A pretty young woman brought coffee to the bar where he sat. He thanked her then asked if she could point out the owner of the newspaper. She directed him to a white haired, distinguished looking man at a table in the far corner, and Dell rose with his coffee to introduce himself.

"Excuse me, sir." He stood beside the table where the man was holding a long, drawn-out conversation with a rather scruffy little character in soiled denim. "I'm sorry to bother you. I'm Sheriff Dell Hoffman from Thomas City. I wonder if I could have a few minutes of your time."

The man frowned at the interruption until he heard Dell was a law-man, after which, he invited him to join them. The newspaper man wore round-rimmed glasses down on his nose. His smile was tight, like he was holding a bullet between his teeth, and he kept looking around, as though wondering who might be listening in on his conversation.

Dell thanked him and slid into a chair across from the man, resting his hat on one knee.

"What is it I can help you with?"

Dell disliked talking to someone whose name he didn't know and won-dered why this gentleman didn't offer that information. He hated to ask for fear it would seem rude. So, he went about it another way. "Well, Mister.... What'd you say your name was? Guess I didn't catch it."

"Oh—uh—sorry." He stuck out his hand. Dell took it, noticing the ink-stains on the man's fingers. Professional hazard, perhaps? "Bryce Truman, owner and publisher of *The Plains Review.* How can I help you?"

Hmm, the man was sort of absent-minded. Something to keep in mind. Dell nodded and settled into his story. "Well, we've had several ranches set afire over the past few months. If that weren't bad enough, the families were all still asleep inside. Some of them didn't wake up in time. I've got a hunch they're being set by a man named Amos Horner, an escaped killer. He's on the vengeance trail after a posse cornered him in his house a few weeks ago, set it afire, and burned up his wife and daughter. He and his older son made it out of the fire. Because he'd escaped prison and was a killer, the posse felt they were right in what they did."

"I remember hearing about that. Terrible thing, just terrible." Truman rubbed his chin. "Do you know for certain it's him?"

"No, but it makes sense. Who else would be motivated to do such a thing? You know, half of finding any criminal is understanding why they choose to do something. Besides, no matter if he's guilty of those crimes or not, he's a convicted killer and a fugitive. Either way, we need to put him back in prison or hang him... which I suspect we should've done in the first place. Anyhow, I'd wondered if you've heard this from any of your residents, or know anything that might give me a lead on this devil? I stopped in at the sheriff's office, but they didn't have much to offer."

Truman shook his head. "I can't say as I have much for you, either, Sheriff, but I'll do a story from your perspective if you'd like. You do understand why we can't write that he committed these fires because you can't prove it. You tell me what you know, and I can quote you."

The scruffy man tapped a finger on the tabletop. "A neighbor of mine was burned out two nights ago, but he and his family was lucky enough to be gone when it happened. You say other people are being burned up in their homes? Who is this Homer fellow? He ought to be hung up by his—"

"Horner. Amos Horn—"

Truman broke in. "No one really knows who's doing it unless someone has seen him carry out the dastardly deed." He addressed Scruffy. "Hank, why wasn't this reported so we could write up a warning in the newspaper? Odd how people don't think along those lines, isn't it?"

He turned to Dell and waited for a reply.

"Yes, sir, it sure is. That's why I'd like you to put something in your paper so those who rode in that posse could be careful. This might be a direct attempt to get back at them. We don't know yet." Dell turned to Scruffy once more. "I wonder if you'd mind giving me these people's names so I could talk to them? Maybe they'd have something to share that would help catch this killer."

Scruffy scratched his beard, where a few breadcrumbs hung. "Tell you what, sir. I'll get in touch with them and see if they might be willing to talk to you. I know they're considering leaving town with what all's going on, but I think they're still around."

Truman cleared his throat. "Maybe they could meet with Sheriff Hoffman at the newspaper office and help him out."

"Oh, I wouldn't share their names 'til I talked to them. You know how folks are about talking to the law."

Truman smiled. "About the same as sharing with the local newspaper, I'd imagine. Why don't you speak to your friends and tell them how important it is that they talk to Sheriff Hoffman here? And then it wouldn't hurt if they dropped in at the newspaper, as well."

Dell gritted his teeth. People round these parts seemed far more interested in helping themselves than helping catch a killer. "Thank you, Mister Truman. I'll be around town most of the day trying to get some information. Could I drop back in at your office later this afternoon, maybe?"

Truman wiped his mouth with a napkin. "You sure could, Sheriff. Now, I'm going to go do some checking of my own. Maybe I'll have some information by the time you come by."

Dell thanked them both, finished his coffee and left. This was not going to be so easy as he'd hoped.

It turned out he was right about that. His return visit to the newspaper gained him nothing but a promise to get in touch if he learned anything.

"That won't be easy, I'll be on the trail for a while trying to run this firebug down. I'll come back through Carlton if I can. If you learn anything of consequence, please send me a wire in Thomas City, if you don't mind."

Truman shook his hand and promised to do that, his eyes straying all over the office. Dell doubted he'd hear from him, even if Horner came in and confessed to him.

THREE

OPEN PLAINS SPREAD AROUND ROSE in every direction, so no matter how long she rode nothing ever changed. After a while it was as if she were standing still. Here a lizard scrambled by, there a sidewinder left a crooked trail in the dust. She didn't even shoot the blamed thing, her mind was so cluttered with the human prey she pursued. This killer was much more dangerous than any rattlesnake that might cross her path.

Dang if she hadn't forgotten all about supplies in her desire to get after that killer. She couldn't even bury her Mama, so who would blame her forgetting such a thing? Now, Carlton was far behind her, and it would be a while before she came to another mercantile or trading post.

Out of sheer frustration, she wanted to kick something, but best not take it out on her faithful horse. It was a big mistake out here in the wild west to let emotions get in the way of caution. But who could blame her? That bastard had burned her mama up without even giving a care. Just wait 'til she caught up with him.

She closed her eyes, remembering the days under Mama's watchful eye running Miss Dottie Lou's House of Pleasure back in Fort Smith. She soon tired of the men and their creepy, crawly hands. Rose half took one man's off when he got too familiar. Her and Mama had a big fight about that. They ended agreeing that Rose needed to find a different calling. Thus, this bounty hunter line of business. Not that Mama approved of that. Not by a long shot. West Texas was a far cry in all respects from Miss Dottie Lou's ruled by Dottie Parsons. Though she learned quickly how to stay out of trouble, Rose still lost her temper far too easily.

Ahead of her, a dust devil rotated up and off the trail startling her from her past back to this dusty, hot, dry, Texas panhandle. A bell was ringing somewhere. She raised up in the stirrups and gazed forward. Dust devils did not make a ringing sound. Out of the wavering haze of heat appeared a wagon. As it drew closer a bell on a stick above the seat came into view. In that seat sat a grizzled old man. Well, maybe not so old, just grizzled. Beard, hair, clothing, all looked like he'd found them in a scrapheap somewhere.

A clatter joined the ringing. Tin pans, plates and cups hung on hooks all in a row below the canvas cover and they rattled along with the rocking of the wagon. He raised an arm, waving a dirty hand at her.

Though she was in dire need of supplies, she almost rode right on by, but he clearly had more than just tinware. The wagon bed sagged with bags of cornmeal, yellow bags of Arbuckle coffee with bright red lettering, beans and other supplies. She couldn't afford to let him pass on by. While the trail was well traveled, he was the first peddler she'd seen. So, she slowed and raised an arm.

"Hello there, selling or buying?"

The small, bearded man, like an elf on the wagon seat, grinned. "Depends entirely, my lass, on your answer to my question." He hauled back on the reins, bringing a single large-footed horse to a snorting standstill.

"Whoa." Cimarron snuffled in reply and stomped a front hoof. No telling what he might be attracted to. "And what might your question be?"

"Are you buying or selling, ma'am?" Eyes closing in merriment, he nodded deeply.

"Clever. I'm in need of some trail supplies, if we could deal right here on the road."

"That indeed is how I deal, Miss." With a nimble leap, he landed on the ground and pulled on a rope that lifted the entire canvas to reveal several shelves filled with all manner of items.

"You, sir, have made me believe in fairies. I just this moment wished for a mercantile to appear like magic, and here you are." Dismounting she chose tin utensils and asked, "Would you have a bag of some sort I could use to carry these wonderful things in? It seems I've set off on a long trip short of the necessities. And would you have a canteen of some sort? I have nothing to carry water if I run across a spring."

"Ah, Miss, you may indeed call me fairy, for I not only have army canvas canteens, I have several filled with water. I can spare one, for I'll soon be at Little Springs and can refill. I must double your cost though. I trust you understand."

"Ah, you're not going to take me for a ride, are you?"

He laughed his funny elf-like laugh. "Now that would be costing you even more, now wouldn't it?"

Sometime later she had two drawstring bags made of flour sacks, paid for with quarter pieces, and in them a cone of brown sugar, a two-pound sack of meal, beans, leavening, salt, a small side of cured bacon, and a bag of Arbuckle's coffee beans, a tin plate, cup, coffee pot and skillet, paid for with six-bits she took from a pouch she carried about her neck. On second thought she added another two bits to make it a dollar. Luck had been with her this time, but next time she'd be more careful and think ahead, even in the worst of conditions. Not too bad a purchase for less than a dollar in paper money. The old man could've skinned her badly had he wanted to.

She had been lucky and waved a good-natured goodbye to which he replied in kind. Still, things could've been worse. How could she have been so foolish as to forget her supplies there beside Mama's burned cabin? What was she thinking? The answer, of course, was revenge, and nothing less.

Added to that was the excitement of spotting two sets of hoof prints leaving the yard, one unusual enough to be easily recognized and followed. Must have put all else out of her mind, but that was no excuse. She could've died.

Going on her way, well supplied, she was sure in her heart that she would find and stop this man who was so evil he burned people in their sleep. Men, women, children. The unusual lightning-struck horseshoe was a happy find. Find that horse and she had one of the men who rode away from the fire at Mama's. Had to be the man she hunted. Only she, of all those who pursued these killers, knew there were two of them. Those had to be the fire starter and his companion. It was impossible there were two sets of outlaws setting fires to houses.

With the sun high in the sky, she munched on jerky from horseback, not stopping to take a dinner break. With spring turning to summer, the Texas sun burned viciously. She and Cimarron worked up a sweat, and she stopped a few times to let the bay rest when they could find shade cast by a tree or boulder.

She was still following the unusual mark. Once in a while, in the soft dust of the trail appeared the mark of a lightning bolt in the hoof prints of two riders. Late in the afternoon they left the trail and headed north toward a line of trees that meant water—probably a small creek or spring. She would be glad for a spring to fill the canteen bought from the peddler but was not prepared to ride up on what could prove to be the men she sought.

So, she held back instead, watching them from the shelter of a boulder 'til they watered and went on their way. They did little talking, but once, the older man shouted in a cruel voice to the boy, who was grown up in size but looked young.

"I tole you over and over, we will get those men who killed yore Ma and little Katie. I won't hear no more, now shut up, boy. Just shut yore mouth."

Rose cringed at the tone and the words. She couldn't help thinking of all the people—some of them kids—that these men had burned to death. If she could get close enough without being seen, she'd put a bullet in the old man's belly, square dab in the middle, and let him lay there and suffer 'til he died hours later. As it was, she would trail them 'til she got the chance, one way or another, to shoot him and carry his head back to the Rangers in Amarillo for her reward. Hell, she'd do it without a reward, he made her so mad.

Nearing sunset, the shadow of a small cabin appeared against the golden horizon. Someone might have seen her quarry. They might have watered there and moved on. The ground had turned rocky, and she'd lost Horner's sign, the lightning bolt, but if he left the trail, she'd see the marks. Surely, he'd remained on the main road. She dared not ride in where he could be lying in wait and get herself shot. But as careful as she'd been, he could have no idea she was following him. The cabin offered the best and safest stop.

A small corral and lean-to barn held some milling cattle — maybe a dozen. A brave start on a herd. Set on stopping, she slowed and watched while a woman came out to draw water from a well, and a man rode up carrying a new calf across the saddle. Mama cow followed, bawling for her baby.

Thoughts of danger overcame Rose. Those devils had pulled up close to this place. Were they going to burn it come midnight when everyone slept? The idea curled the edges of her thoughts of Mama lying in piles of ashes, and others the same. If she were careful, she could put an end to this right here. Tonight. Those two weren't the only ones who could attack in the dark.

She reined Cimarron up and studied the landscape around the small farm. Not many places to hide. She could warn those folks, then help them protect their place, but that might be dangerous for the couple. Perhaps it was best to go in search of the burners' camp and slay them while they slept. They could be lying in wait inside there, but things sure looked normal, and the dirt carried no sign of the funny marked horseshoe.

Oh, how she itched to ride in on them, guns blazing 'til they lay dead in their own blood so they would know who had killed them. Too iffy. One of them could cut her down. Or they might not be there. Her imagination had sort of run away with her. Everything had to be just right for her to take them both down.

However, the chance they'd made camp for the night was a good one, since it was getting on dusk now. Best to wait and surprise them, in this camp or the next, while they lay on their blankets snoring away. It would mean going on for a while after she picked up that lightning bolt mark again, in case she had been seen, then coming back after dark to carry out her deeds.

Yes, that would be best. Then she could leave their bodies—well everything but the older one's head—claim her reward and ride on into New Mexico for a while. Pick up some wanteds there to go after. Sheriff Hoffman was an honorable man who might call such actions murder and feel he had to come after her. They had clashed before, but she had always slipped away keeping her actions legal, or if not, then not provable as downright murder.

Even if she made camp a good mile past the small cabin, she debated what might be her wisest choice. No sign of the sheriff on the trail of these men. Perhaps she ought to challenge them, shoot them down and haul their ugly heads back to Thomas City where she could claim the reward posted for the fire starter. Maybe even demand more reward since there were two of them.

One was a young boy, though. She had forgotten that.

Surely, he didn't deserve killing. She couldn't kill a child, even if Horner had. From what she'd overheard, the boy didn't agree with what his pa was doing.

Soon, she came upon a small spring, rare in the panhandle, but existing if you searched, and after checking around, set up her camp there where she could see the trail approaching from both directions.

She would eat, get her thoughts straight and pick up the trail first thing. Once the fire had hot coals, she sliced some bacon into the tin skillet, mixed up corn meal, salt, leavening, and water and dropped two blobs to fry in the fat cooked out of the bacon. Coffee boiled in the small tin pot. It was the kind of meal she was accustomed to while on the move. Come a couple of weeks of trail eating, she'd crave a nice juicy steak with a side serving of potatoes and gravy.

Before she could take a sip of the coffee, something rustled in the leaves under a small spread of trees nearby. She dropped the cup, pawed her gun free and hit the dirt on her belly.

"Don't come no further or I'll shoot."

"Don't shoot my dog. Please. I'll take him home. Please?"

A kid. A doggone kid and his dog. She came close to laughing at herself, but when you thought how close she came to shooting first then asking questions, the snicker died in her throat.

"Kin I just get my dog and go home?"

She put away the gun and scrambled to her feet. "Git your dog, but don't sneak up on someone like that again. You could've got shot."

The child came closer. He wore striped overalls with no shirt and had blond curls to his shoulders and the prettiest blue eyes. His bare toes were muddy from wading in water. Well, dammit, she'd been seen now. No getting out of it.

"Son, go ahead, catch the mutt and hightail it home. It's almost dark. What you doing out this late?"

"I—I'm not a son. I'm a—a girl. Whatcha doing out here yourself? It's almost dark." The girl put her hands on her hips and gave Rose a cute smirk.

"Smart one, huh? I'm big enough to be out after dark, you aren't. What would your mama think?"

The child shrugged. "She was crying and told me to come outside for a while, and Spot there ran away. So, I came to get him and found you."

Rose, this is none of your business. Still, she couldn't keep her mouth shut. "Why was Mama crying? Did she get hurt or something?"

"Daddy got mad and he smacked her, and she fell on the floor."

Well, dammit. Just dammit. What was she supposed to do now?

ROSE CONSIDERED THE DOG, THEN the little girl. Rising from the

campfire, she tightened the belt of her leather holster holding the Colt and
took the girl's hand.

"So, what's your name?"

"Amelia, but Mama calls me Amy."

"Well, come on then, let's go see your mama." She pulled a briskly burning limb from the fire. The child might make her way on a pitch-black
night, but she wasn't about to try it. Walking up on a rattlesnake or falling
in a hole didn't appeal to her.

"Don't tell my daddy I said that about him hitting Mama."

Before Rose could reply to the pitiful request a burning log broke sending sparks into the night sky. Amy pointed and, in a voice still filled with
tears, spoke. "Pretty. Wishes to angels."

Rose watched the pinpoints of fire dance through the darkness 'til they
faded. How wonderful if such childhood beliefs could be right. But that was
foolish. Holding the torch high, she took a few steps, and Amy ran to keep
up. Back to reality.

"Does he hit your Mama a lot?"

"What's a lot?"

Rose's temper, the one she worked so hard to keep in check, boiled up
from deep inside 'til her face grew hot and her heart beat fast. What in hell
was she doing? She couldn't stop this but one way, and that wouldn't solve
Amy's problem, nor in the end her own. Why did she care anyhow? If only
she hadn't stopped here. If only the child had stayed away. If only that ass-
hole hadn't burned Mama's cabin down, so she had to come after him. So
many if-onlys she couldn't count them.

By then she had stomped her way to the porch steps of the cabin, the
child's hand held firmly in hers. Though it was dark, no lamp had come on
inside. She could pretend she'd never been here, open the door, push the
little girl in and leave. No, what if he'd killed the woman? What would she

do if he had? Now, there she went with all the what ifs. She dropped the burning limb in the bare yard. Stop, go in, do something.

She knelt beside Amy, so their faces were on a level. "Honey, I want you to wait right here while I go talk to your mama and daddy. Can you do that?"

Amelia nodded, plopped down on the step and hugged her dog close. It licked her face and made her giggle. Good, that was good.

She went onto the porch and peered through the open door. There was no glass in the window holes and the sound of the woman sobbing carried out into the night. At least she was alive. Rose sucked in a deep sigh of relief.

From out in the woods an owl hooted once, twice, three times. Another replied. Some believed that meant a death was imminent. More foolishness. It was merely two owls talking, arranging a rendezvous. Time to go inside. Straightening, Rose rapped hard on the open door. What would she say? Or do? Easy to know what she wanted. Shoot the bastard and let it all sort out.

She glanced down at Amy who in turn looked up at her, blue eyes shining with tears. Slowly, Rose stepped through the doorway. "Hello? Anyone home?"

Only the sobbing from inside. Another step. "You all right?"

A match flared giving off the familiar smell of sulphur, and a lamp came on in the corner of the room. "What in hell you doing in my house?" A man's coarse voice.

Heart in her throat, she jumped at the anger of the question, pulled the gun partway out. Reconsidered. Finally stuttered a reply. "Sorry, I was camping down the trail and found your dog. I brought him home. Gave him to your little girl. Out on the porch. Sorry, just wanted to make sure everything was okay." She had to lie. The tone in his words told her so.

He emerged from the shadows, a large man who needed clean clothes, a shave, and a haircut. "Though you did me no favor returning the mutt, you thought it fine to step into my house?"

The sound of the woman crying carried clear after he stopped shouting.

She hadn't let go of the gun, her thumb rubbing the pearl handle. Shit, she wanted to shoot him so bad. Haul him in over the back of a horse and claim he tried to kill her.

"Is someone in there hurt?" She glared up, struggled to see his fierce features No luck. In the shadows cast by the lamplight neither could see more than a silhouette of the other.

"None of your business. You brought the dog home, don't give you rights to butt in. Now you can be on your way."

"If you don't mind, I'd like to make sure she's not hurt." The gun slid slick as you please into her fist and the barrel caught a glint from the moon that peeked above the horizon. She had it pointed into his face. "If you don't mind." She repeated those words sharply.

Venom colored his expression. He snarled and took a quick step back.

Easy to see he would kill her if he could get his hands on her safely. She slid along the wall but away from him further into the house. Out of his reach, stay out of his reach.

"Show me and I'll leave. I mean it, mister."

He nodded, walked in front of her. "You're gonna be sorry for this."

"Maybe, maybe not. Where is she?"

"In on the bed. She fell that's all."

"Okay. Does she need help? Could you light a lamp in there so I can see?"

"Got to go into the room. Don't reckon she's hurt, didn't ask."

"Show me."

The scratch and again that sulphur smell tickled her nostrils. With a flare of light, the wick flickered to life inside the smoky glass. The flame created dancing figures in the gloomy room, and it was difficult to see well. He could jump her at any moment if he chose.

"Call out to her, if you don't mind." Why was she being so polite to this man who obviously was a wife beater? "Ma'am, are you all right?" She halted, no longer able to see the man who had shuffled into a dark corner. He posed danger. Curled around the gun butt, her hand shook. Pull it or not?

"Yes, yes, I'm fine." The weak feminine voice stilled her movements.

Didn't sound fine, but she was alive. Now what? She wanted to tell the woman to pack up her things, get on as horse with Amy and ride into town. Get on a stage and go back home to her folks. But no matter how she felt, this was not her business, and if the woman wanted to stay here, she would do so. Rose could only make matters worse. And so was the way of the world.

"Your little girl is out here, and she needs you. Could you tell me you are able to care for her, and I'll go on my way?"

Before she could even guess what would happen next the woman leaped off the bed, shoved her aside and started screaming. Foul words that shocked even Rose who had pretty much heard them all. The gist of her demands was that Rose go away, mind her own business, not try to tell her how to raise her child or deal with her man.

It was enough for Rose. She backed away, holstered her gun and left. Behind her the man shouted, "And don't come back neither 'less you want shot yourself."

In patches of moonlight Rose fled into the night, stumbled toward the flickering flames of her campfire burning in the distance. That would certainly teach her to mind her own business, at least once in a while. Though she carried worries about the woman and child with her, she could do nothing further for them. They would have to do that themselves.

If nothing else, the fire reminded her why she was out here. What she needed to concentrate on. So, she went back to what she did the best herself. Pursuing those two devils 'til she caught them and hauled them in to the nearest law office to collect the bounty, like she'd set out to do in the first place. And to hell with the rest of the world. This was hers, and she had learned quite well how to deal with it.

Fearful that the man left behind in the cabin might sneak up on her in the night and beat her senseless, she silently packed up, threw dirt on the fire and moved on past the now-lit house almost a mile before she found a new camp. For a long time, she lay awake watching the egg-shaped moon slip quietly across the sky.

It wasn't that she was afraid so much as she was careful not to submit herself to obvious dangers. Mama had taught her that years earlier when she entertained at Dottie Lou's in Ft. Smith. Those lessons served her well when she had to deal with a man like that one. Once she had enough and saw that the man she was with was going to kill her, she'd reversed the situation. And since going into the bounty business the knowing kept her alive. Thus, she ran from a man she could've easily killed. The wife-beating bastard would pay one day, most surely. When his angry wife decided she'd had enough and took care of the matter herself.

Unable to sleep very much, Rose finally gave up and rose as soon as it was light enough to track. She didn't bother with breakfast, but packed, saddled up and climbed on an objecting Cimarron who stood hip-shot and sleeping until she slipped the bridle over his nose. He tossed his head and whinnied.

"Here boy, you're getting as skittish as me. Sorry I scared you." She rubbed the velvety nose until the large horse settled down. Even so he stomped to let her know it was much too early to light out. Or that's what she thought was the matter 'til a voice said her name.

"Rosie, darlin'. It's just me."

Before he could go on, she had her gun pulled, and had whirled to point it in his direction.

"You done shot me one time, don't make it two." He moved to where she could make out who it was. There he stood, the man she thought she'd never see again.

"Travis? My God, Travis Dockery. I thought—" She dropped the reins to the ground, palmed her gun.

"Yes, it's me and I know what you thought, but they let me out. Said I was too nice a guy to keep in prison."

She uncurled her fingers from the butt of the Colt and took a step or two but stopped. "How did you find me?"

"Why I asked around. Anyone sees you never forgets you."

"And why? I hope you didn't come to get back at me."

He laughed in the way she remembered, a way that once sent goose bumps up her spine.

"Why, honey babe, you're too sweet to shoot. That'd be a darned waste. Come here."

She looked around like someone might be watching, or perhaps he was talking to someone else. Then unable to hold back any longer she ran and jumped into his arms. He caught her easily, all six feet of her. A man big enough to do that and then some.

Nose buried in his neck. He smelled so good, like leather and honeysuckle and early morning dew. She slid from his arms before getting carried away anymore. "And just why did you look for me? You surely didn't want to get shot again. Or hauled off to jail. I got paid plenty for turning you in."

He gazed down at her. "Sure, but you didn't chop off my head and carry it in for the money, now did you? I considered that to mean you cared something for me."

"I'd a cared a lot more if you didn't rob banks. How long you been out? Obviously not long enough to get on the wanted list again." Being around this man for long was dangerous. She backed out of his reach, keeping a weary eye upon him.

"I've been behaving myself, but I heard something really terrible up in Carlton. About that yahoo burning folks up? I can't tolerate anyone who'd do that. You know I've never hurt anyone."

She covered his lips with her fingertips. "Now wait... you shot that man in Amarillo when he tried to stop you robbing his bank."

"Yeah, but I just winged him, and he shot me back worse. I was laid up with Jake and his bunch for nearly a month before I got on the road again."

"Okay, so why are you really here?"

"Just to see you, I promise. But I thought I'd get in on chasing down this fire starter. I'm not wanted by anyone, so it'd be all legal and everything. I figure a lot of rangers and deputies are in on it. And knew you would be, so that's what I'm doing here. Can I go along? Please? I'll behave myself. I hear Jake is thinking of joining in too. This guy is giving men like us a bad name. Plus, a five thousand dollar bounty ain't nothing to sneeze at."

She leaned against him, stared up into his cobalt blue eyes, so dark they nearly looked black 'til the light caught them just so. How could a man born so gorgeous be so blamed ornery? If she stayed around him too long, she'd be in trouble. He was the only man she'd ever met that she couldn't resist since losing her husband who'd gone off to war and never come back. Maybe that's why she'd shot him and took him in for a reward. She'd hoped that would get her over him—but it didn't.

One look at him now and she shook her head at her own weakness. It hadn't gotten her over him at all, not in the least.

"So, it's up to five thousand? A fine chunk of change. Okay, if you can convince Sheriff Hoffman and any other lawmen involved, I don't mind you riding along. And I've no doubt you can. You could charm squirrels out of trees. I know you're a good gun hand but be careful. You do something wild and crazy, and I'll shoot you again. I have a feeling I could make a good living taking you in for bounty.

He shook his head, long hair shining like mahogany in the early morning light, his laughter making her spirit sing. That was the trouble with being around Trav. He left her knees weak and her heart hammering. And she didn't know what to do about it short of shooting him.

FOUR

THERE WAS MORE THAN ONE way to hunt down a snake in the grass, so leaving Curly and the mule tied in front of the Carlton sheriff's office, Dell walked down the street a way to the Kick 'Em High Saloon. If anyone had seen anything today it might be someone having a beer and staring out the swinging doors, a little bored and a lot talkative. If there was anything he hated, it was wasting time chasing after someone who'd gone the other way. So, just to make sure, he'd ask around before heading out. Hope someone had spotted a suspicious stranger with the stench of death on him.

Might not be too many in there yet this time of the day, but there were always a few bellied up to the bar day or night. Turned out he didn't have to go inside, after all. In front of the barber and bath shop next to the saloon someone had conveniently placed a bench, and on that bench sat a fellow with white hair who could've used the barber shop, but that wasn't Dell's business.

He stopped. The man glanced up. A dust devil twisted down the center of the dirt street and both men watched 'til it settled.

"Howdy, mind if I sit a spell?"

"Surely don't. Uh—ain't seen you around town before."

"Been here a few times, just riding through though."

The older man smiled. "And are you just riding through today, or have you decided to stop for a while?"

"Stopping a while. Name's Dell Hoffman."

"That'd be *Sheriff* Dell Hoffman."

"I know you?"

"Nope. I read your badge there on your coat."

"How very astute of you."

They shared a laugh.

He stuck out a hand. "Name's Ned Yingling. And what can I do for you today, Sheriff?"

"To tell the truth, you look like someone who notices what's going on around him, and I need to know about that very thing."

"That very thing being what goes on in this fine town."

"Exactly. I see I'm right about your astuteness."

"Ask away. You'll find I'm filled with it. Astuteness that is. Good word, that."

"Ah. Yes, indeed. Would you have noticed anyone passing through who didn't seem to belong? Who might have been up to some chicanery? Or looked like they were fleeing? I know that's a lot to ask, but not if you've been astute."

"You might say that more than one could've fit that bill as to chicanery. Another fine word, that. Do you have any description at all?"

"I can tell you it could've been yesterday coming on late or maybe this morning. This someone has torched homes while people slept in them, so he probably has no heart or soul, or perhaps is the meanest bastard walking this earth. He likely has a younger lad with him."

"Is there a wanted poster out on this heartless, soulless person?"

"Maybe for another crime, no one has seen him in the act, but he is wanted for escaping jail. There is a huge bounty on him now suspicioning him of arson. They plan on proving it later. If you got close to him, a definite stench would be present."

Ned stared into the street. "Proving it by hanging him? My last question before I search my memory. Could he be a part of a gang or more than one person?"

"Superb question. I'm not seeing him as a gang member. Just a gut feeling, 'cause the scene of the last fire was pretty tore up by lawmen's horses. Still, you know how that goes." He patted his stomach. "I'm searching for one, or no more than two men."

Ned searched his memory for a long while and Dell waited patiently. There was always some hope.

But the old man shook his head and met Dell's close stare. "Sure sorry, but I can't come up with anything, but I'll keep my eyes open and tell it around town. You have a poster up?"

"Not one of the killer, but it's time we get one posted. Reward's gone to five thousand. Someone may already know the feller. Thanks for your help." He reached out a hand.

The old man placed his gnarly fingers in Dell's palm. "Good to meet you. Hope you get that un, he sounds like he needs killing."

Back where he'd left his animals, Dell went inside the sheriff's office, hoping he'd find someone besides the youngster. He did. It happened the town marshal, Ben Brewster, had dropped by and they discussed a reward for the fire starter and getting posters printed up. Dell promised that Saddler County would kick in on expenses on both.

The marshal frowned. "We have to stop this. Who ever heard of such a thing? Takes a mighty ornery animal to kill in such a way. Have to wonder what he gets out of it. These people don't have much for him to steal 'fore he sets the fire. Must be doing it for his sick enjoyment."

"You're right. I've been trying to figure him out, why he does what he does. Reckon we'll have to ask him, if we can take him alive. I've got a theory but no proof. If you want to go ahead with the poster and reward arrangements and send my county it's share of the bill, I'd be obliged. I'm headed west, not figuring he'd head east into the arms of the US Marshals in Indian Territory. I'm trying to find sign of this man. Maybe I'll get lucky and catch him in the act."

The town marshal scratched his ear and tilted his head a bit. "Reckon you've considered taking a look in Palo Duro. Outlaws sometimes gather there coming and going. Anyhow, I'll keep an eye out, and you let me know. We'll try to keep things closed down good here and watch out for such."

They said goodbye, and Dell left Carlton none the wiser than when he arrived. Good deal they had Ben Brewster, what with the sheriff's deputy being so surly. He studied the Guadalupe mountains reaching for the sky along the western horizon. Ever danged owl hoot who pulled dirty business in the panhandle if they didn't hole up in the canyon, made for those mountains to hide out. That was the other place the marshal had mentioned, but he'd have to detour to make sure. Best to scour this part of the Panhandle first.

Surprised why he hadn't thought of checking out Palo Duro. That was a good piece of advice. He might lose any time he'd gained, but something in his gut told him to heed that suggestion. Those two boys who rode out of Miz Parson's place this morning looked familiar, and now he knew why. They'd rode in a bunch of outlaws the posse had run out of the canyon a few months ago. Sometimes, men like that were likely to know what was going on with other bunches that rode outside the law. And, once in a while, they'd talk if there might be something in it for them. Like not getting arrested.

Cutting across the plains on a little-used trail, he made for the canyon. It was a big place, next to the Grand Canyon in size, but much of it was Goodnight's ranch. Those ranch hands spent their time in the saddle on the range. Outlaws preferred the bluffs and caves. Best to make sure before he traveled on. Lord, those two yahoos could be anywhere.

After another long day's ride that took him within a day's trip of Palo Duro, he camped within the adobe ruins of a house. A cold wind had raised off the mountains, and he welcomed the shelter of the walls. Early spring and those mountains could bring some danged brutal weather that often swept across the plains.

With the extra ground cover he'd brought, he snugged down, tied the animals in the shelter with him and had barely laid his head on his saddle when the sound of galloping horses filled the cold night air. At the noise he yanked his rifle from the scabbard and hunkered into the shadowy corner of the adobe to wait and watch. The moonlight, bright as day, showed him six or seven riders who rode right on past as if the shelter weren't there. Obviously, they had hurried business elsewhere.

Curiosity gnawed at him, but he had to stick to his own business. Couldn't go chasing after every fleeing rider, but he sure couldn't help but wonder what had them skedaddling across the plains so blamed fast.

Being a lawman made him naturally nosy, and he fussed around his camp, unable to go back to sleep. The huge old moon didn't help any either. When he did lay down on his bedroll, he imagined his own bed with beautiful Guinn lying beside him, warming him from the cold wind.

He laughed at his silliness. If he were in his own bed, there wouldn't be any cold wind, and he could smell the rose water on the sheets. Her nightgown would slip off one shoulder when he laid his hand on her hip. Eyes drooping closed in his lonely bedroll, he moved to take her up on the invite.

FIVE

TRAV KEPT AN ARM AROUND Rose a long time. "Don't see why I can't just go with you to catch this bandit. We catch him I trust you to share the bounty with me."

Still feeling the unwanted attraction to this man who held such influence over her, Rose slipped from his embrace. "You think I'd trust you to share? You'd manage to make off with the entire purse and me looking right at you."

"Aw, Rosie darlin', you don't really believe that?"

"I sure do, 'cause you've done it before. Stay on my coattails while I track someone down, then talk me into sharing, or take off while I'm sleeping, taking it all with you."

He kissed her cheek, then moved to pounce on her lips. She pushed him away.

"Go on now. You want to help the lawmen bring this man in, be my guest, but get their permission to ride with 'em. Maybe they'll deputize you."

He laughed. "Are you kidding? Well, I guess I'll just go out on my own and put a stop to his burning. Then you'll see. I might even come back and share some of the reward with you 'cause you steered me toward it."

"Ha, Trav. Just Ha. Now go on, git, before I take up target practice on your gorgeous ass."

An hour or so later, after eating breakfast together beside a campfire, Trav pulled a sad face, saddled his black horse, and rode away.

Well, congratulations, Rose. You finally have some sense about that handsome no-good. Never mind the strange loss that left her feeling empty watching him disappear down the trail. But she refused to be like Mama and bed him only to find herself alone with a child to raise. Mama had always resented Rose, as if it were she who caused the trouble of caring for a child while making a living on her own. The man she wanted was one who would marry her, live with her in a real house, and come home every night. Love was for saps. Especially the kind she felt for that no-good Trav. And it would last as long as a June frost.

Thinking such thoughts to console herself she saddled Cimarron and rode carefully along the trail, crisscrossing to make sure she didn't miss the shoe and its special mark. The thing about tracking was to look away from the disturbed trail to find the one time the horse stepped off into the unmarked soil on either side of the trail. Or a clump of grass broken down by one hoof-print carrying that lightning bolt mark. Finding it in a heavily traveled trail was nigh impossible.

It was almost noon before she picked up where a horse had strayed off the trail for several feet. Perhaps the rider either dozed off or was looking away and let him step in the smooth earth several times.

But there it was, the mark that spelled doom for him. She'd see him caught, dead or alive, for the dastardly deeds. Sending his black soul to hell was her only concern, and until it was done, she wouldn't stop this pursuit. Though she hoped to be the one to do it, for who wouldn't want the bounty that went along with the satisfaction, as long as it was done, she'd be content.

Anyway, he was still following the main trail, and when or if he left it, she'd see that too. Jake had taught her well from when they were kids. He'd leave a vague trail then set her out to try to follow it, going with her to point out what was right and wrong. By the time they were grown and him gone off to war, she was an experienced tracker.

And while she was working for Mama over in Fort Smith, the well-known owner of a huge ranch in Texas, who visited Dottie Lou's regularly, took a liking to Rose. To show his appreciation he presented her with a running wild two-year old Andalusian bay she named Cimarron. Sixteen hands high to match her extraordinary height, he said. She tamed him enough to climb on his back and ride with the wind. Days off, she'd light out for Indian Territory astride that big Andalusian galloping full-out. The two of them, wild as wild could be. One day, she met up with an outlaw dragging a bloody young girl across the red dirt of Indian Territory. She became a bounty hunter that day, returned the child to her parents and presented his head to a marshal in Fort Smith. She walked away with five hundred dollars, quit Dottie Lou's that evening and moved to Texas where she claimed there were plenty more outlaws that needed killing.

The animal wearing a lightning bolt marked horseshoe and his companion moved off the main trail noontime the second day. Rose followed his tracks. Where were they going and for what? On the way to burn another homestead? They couldn't be too far ahead of her. She found signs of their overnight camping plus stops twice to water and rest horses.

On the third day, she was both happy and disappointed to ride up on a small Mexican trading post. A few scrawny trees grew around the place, like there might be water underground, though none was visible anywhere. As she feared, she lost the tracks among those of burros, mules, horses, and wagons that had come and gone in the churned, rutted dirt around the adobe building and hitching rails. Odd how busy the place was, but she'd take things as they came.

On the good side of things, it was nice to get a chance to rest her sore bottom. Sliding to the ground she tied Cimarron where she could keep an eye on him from inside and trooped in hoping to get herself something to drink, wet if not cold, and maybe learn about an outlaw on the loose easier to catch than the lightning duo. Dragging back one with a bounty posted would help add to her diminishing pocketbook. The peddler had thinned out her cash some.

A sign over the counter welcomed her to Ojo which meant eye. How creepy that was. The place was half mercantile, half bar and the smells of feed, beer and cigar smoke mingled together in a sour way. She ordered a shot of the house whiskey followed by a warm beer.

Even when she wore britches and tucked her long sun-streaked hair up under her Stetson, she was still never taken for a man. Being shapely in womanly places ran in the family. Sometimes that wasn't a good thing, but here, no one seemed to mind a woman bellied up to the bar.

A beautiful Mexican girl stood toward the back singing something lovely in Spanish, Rose's favorite language for music. She leaned against the counter and listened, eyes half closed.

From outside came a huge ruckus, riders shouting and laughing, a gun going off. She raised her head just enough to see over the swinging doors. A place like this with no law to speak of, no one paid much attention to anyone else unless there was a killing. And she wasn't interested in taking someone in who had no price on their head. Let 'em have at it, long as they left her and her kind alone. Meaning women and kids of course.

The few customers either at the bar or buying supplies glanced up as if the noise was an expected disturbance, then went on about their business. Though no one else seemed aroused, Rose slid 'til her back was against the side wall and laid one hand over the top of the Colt holstered at her right side. The new arrivals stomped in, four men and two youngsters maybe fourteen or so. All swaggered and carried guns on their hips, like they were William Bonney or someone, plus two of the men also had a rifle in their other hand. These men were tough and meant everyone to know it.

They filled the bar and she listened as best she could. Sometimes men like these bragged about what they did or who they knew. They always figured they were cocks of the walk, and no one would dare

mess with them. At first, they got their drinks, kept a bottle to continue filling their glasses and, just as she thought, began to spout to each
other about their prowess.

For a while she listened halfway, not really interested in who did what
to who, but then one of them said, "You can't blame Horner for it. Hell,
he'd married, settled down, wanted no part of the bunch anymore, but the
law blamed him for a killing down in Lubbock."

"Yeah, I heard he'd never ever been that far from home."

"True, but the posse burned him and his family out, killed his wife and
new baby and a boy staying with them was burnt real bad. He recovered.
Bad doings."

"I'd say bad doings. Can't blame him one bit. I'd do the same."

"They'll catch him, though, and when they do, he'll hang."

"Have there been any more ranch burnings?"

"Not in the last few days. Burned out that ole gal who used to own a
saloon. Why, if it's only revenge, they did that I'll never know. Maybe she
was just in the way."

Another swigged down a double shot. "I heard she was some kin to a
bounty hunter. Maybe the guy is just cleaning up as he sees fit."

The men shook their heads, poured another round from the bottle and
went on to other subjects.

Shocked to the core, she wanted only to get out of there. Could it be
true? Could it be her fault Mama was burned? The way she'd heard it,
Horner had escaped from prison after killing a lawman in Lubbock. He hid
out at his house where the posse did try to burn him out. And it did burn
up his wife and baby. Plenty of motivation to go to burning up them who'd
done it. But Mama had nothing to do with it. And neither did Rose.

But what if they were right about the motivation of these burnings? It
was all just conjured up so as to blame this Horner fella. Still, she would
continue to pursue him and his friend because it was the best clue she had
to the identification of the arsonists.

Shaking, she kept her eyes pointed down, hoping to hear more. The talker shut up when a man rode in yelling something she couldn't understand. Everyone ran out and surrounded him. He spoke in Spanish so she could only understand a few words, but one was caliente and the other tres muerta. Men scattered and soon a group rode out. A fire. It must be another ranch or homestead burning. She followed at a distance. Against the distant horizon smoke trailed high into the sky.

Fire in the open spaces of west Texas and New Mexico often meant complete destruction and death. There were very few ways to fight a barn or house fire other than a bucket brigade. That took people and water from a tank or nearby horse trough.

By the time she arrived with the crowd, the inside of the adobe ranch house had been entirely gutted. A pole barn nearby had some hay smoking inside. Two wild-eyed horses were being held a way out in the pasture.

Rose dismounted and stood close to a cluster of men hoping to get more information. If it were an outlaw gang that burned out the man and boy who were said to be going around setting the fires, then how did the guilty ones own ranches? Outlaws seldom owned more than their horse, often stolen, and a pair of worn boots. This didn't make sense.

A lot of Spanish was spoken which she didn't understand. At last, she figured out enough to complete the tale she'd heard earlier in Ojo. The man doing the burning was accused of killing a marshal over in Lubbock, so a posse went after him. He claimed he didn't do it, fought back and killed a deputy marshal. That's all she heard before the conversation took a turn. Some of the men lost their temper and a fight broke out over the man's guilt.

Someone noticed her and started her way as if they thought she didn't belong. Uh-oh. Time she lit out before things turned violent. The best thing to do was mount up and ride off, and so she did. Evidently the crowd was more interested in the fire than in chasing her. With what little information she had, she might learn more, but not here from these people on the verge of hysteria. They were looking for any stranger they could hang from the nearest tree, and she didn't want to be one of them. Shouting and gunplay continued while she rode away searching for signs of the familiar horseshoe.

WARY OF BEING SHOT AT, Dell dismounted before reaching Palo Duro, which wasn't easy to calculate, seeing as how you couldn't see the canyon 'til you were ready to fall over the rim. Unless you had your bearings, so to speak. Anyway, it was middle of the afternoon of the second day before he reached a few saplings growing in a peculiar pattern. These were used as landmarks by those familiar with the lay of the land. The canyon was a few minutes on down the trail and offered not only a spot to tie Curly, but he couldn't be seen approaching.

Swinging to the ground with the Remington rifle in his left hand, he started walking. He'd had time to do some thinking after deciding to check out the canyon. Best if he went in without a badge, more like a lone rider looking to dodge the law. Still might be smart to do some sneaking and not ride right up on whoever might be there. So, he'd also left his Stetson safely hung on the saddle horn 'cause it was so danged new it automatically looked suspicious.

He'd be one against who knew how many which made him extra careful, so he approached in bits and spurts. A cool wind blew across from the mountains, drying the sweat where his shirt clung to his chest. The trail leading into this particular section of the huge canyon was steep, rocky and narrow. He circled around making sure there weren't any guards evident. If any of the gangs were in hiding, there'd be one just below the rim behind a cliff, boulder or crop of hardwood trees for which Palo Duro was named.

Just walking down the rocky incline would make noise, so better to take his time. Creeping along made him feel a bit ridiculous, but he sure didn't want to get shot. Once in a while, he stopped cold and listened close.

It was a long way to the bottom. Some claimed this canyon was second in size and depth to the Grand Canyon. That was probably true, though he'd never traveled the width and depth of it. It was pretty dang wide and deep so that could be true.

He was nearly to the bottom and beginning to breathe easier when he heard someone clear his throat and laugh. Felt like he was right on top of him. A jutting of rock just ahead offered a small hole just big enough for him to scoot into. Holding the rifle straight up and down in front of him, he waited. If whoever was coming looked his way at the right time, he'd see him. But the trail being rugged as it was, chances are he'd be paying attention to where he was walking.

An outlaw running up against a sheriff with an obvious badge on would point and shoot with no hesitation. Other outlaws would come running, so he couldn't be ready to do the same without being mowed down. He held his breath and let the footsteps crunch on by. The man was alone, didn't even have his horse. Just out for a stroll, looking around. No telling what for. They might've thought they heard him. One thing for sure, his heart beat so loud the old boy was bound to turn and look.

Hell, he'd stopped. Right in front of him. Back to him, staring out across the rim of the canyon. Go on, git where you were going 'fore I fart or sneeze or something stupid.

"Aw, ain't no one up there." Boots sliding on the steep gravel, the fellow went back down the path, his hat disappearing from view at last.

By the time he made his cautious way to the bottom the sun had slid partway across the sky. No one challenged him.

Just about when he believed he'd been careful enough not to be heard or spotted, a gun barrel drilled into his back. Damn it all. He jumped, stooped and laid the rifle on the ground. Well, at least they hadn't shot him. Yet.

"Hold it there. Just what do you want?"

"Taking me a walk in this beautiful country. Looking is all."

"Yeah, sure. And chickens lay golden eggs."

A hand roughly pulled his handgun from its holster. Next thing he came back to himself near a campfire in the dark of night amidst a bunch of rowdy men. His head felt like someone had bounced a good-sized rock off it a few times.

He couldn't help it, he moaned. Better if he hadn't, but shit, his head was killing him. Now they knew he'd come to.

"Well, lookee here, our visitor's done come around. Have a good sleep, did you?" The man whacked him across the head with an open palm, and stars flew in every direction.

"Now, don't go doing that." That was someone else, so that made two of them.

"You wanna kill him 'fore we find out who he is and what he wants?"

Ah, someone standing up for him. Maybe he had a chance after all. Dell folded both arms across his head. Tried to talk but nothing but mush-mouth came out. So, he settled his face in the crook of his bent elbows and took some deep breaths.

"Give him time to come around this time, you blamed idjit. I for one want to know how the law found us down here."

"For your information, he didn't find us, I found him 'fore he could."

Maybe he was in luck. Only two men so far. The first one who'd whacked him had a deep voice, the other a bit younger, it seemed.

"I come near to shooting him when I first seen him sneaking around."

Dell raised his head. "Might ask a man what he wants before you try to kill him. I'm a friend of a fella who used to run with a bunch who hid out down here. Hoped I'd still find 'em."

"Law ain't a friend. A fella? A bunch? Being sorta vague there. Give us a name, you might save your own life."

"Mac Brown was the fella." Damn, he'd grabbed the first outlaw's name he could remember putting away. Hoped he was out by now.

"Wait, I heered of him. Rode with him oncet long time ago."

Well, dang. A new voice to the conversation. Dell squinted into the shadows beyond the firelight. He was gonna get himself killed, sure as the world. Might as well keep it up as long as he could get away with it.

A bow-legged, half-bald man shuffled over. "Name's Dynamite Johnson."

Dell offered his hand. "Sure, Brown talked about you a lot. Said you was hell with a stick of blow."

Dynamite did a little heel-kicking dance. "Sure, reckon you're his cousin, Pole."

Dell grabbed onto the name. "Short for Poleaxed. Got hit in the head when I was a kid and they called me that from then on. Say, I sure hope you thought to fetch my Remington. Would sure hate to lose that."

"He never told me that, but it sounds just like the other stuff he never told me about you. Like you was a lawman."

Dell flicked at the badge. "Took this off a feller I found drunk and laying on the ground beside his horse. You like it, you can have it." He unfastened the badge and held it out.

Dynamite grabbed the badge. "Thankee. Hell, Greasy, give this man a cup of coffee and a plate of beans. He's family."

And if they bought *that* flimsy lie, they were dumber than a sack of dirt. "My rifle?"

"Oh, about that rolling block. I sure have fancied me one of them. I thank you for toting in down here to me"

Well, hell. He'd have to see about that. Couldn't lose that Remington to one of these slugs. He ate the beans and slurped the coffee without further comment while the others talked and laughed, smoked and argued about past and future deeds.

A big ole boy took his empty plate and sat down beside Dell. "Say, how come you to be hunting this Mac Brown?"

"I heard he got caught up in a posse couple weeks ago, some said they were hunting this fella who's been setting fires and killing folk. I'd hate it if they got good old Mac Brown."

The big man settled down to one side on a stump. "That's something, ain't it? We been dodging them posse fellas ever whipstitch. They's the ones started it in the first place. Burned up his wife and little kid. Now that there ain't right, no matter what he done."

The man was right. What had driven a sworn-in posse to do such a thing? Hard to figure. They ought to be brought in right along with the fire starter, who hadn't ought to be doing what he was either. Often times, the law had to sort out some mighty confusing stuff. But he'd haul them all in if he had his way. If he ever got himself out of this, that is.

Didn't seem like the men he wanted were here, so his best bet was to sneak off in the middle of the night and head back home to Thomas City. After, by God, he retrieved his rifle. Maybe someone back there had gone on to learn some more about this arsonist. They had to catch him before he did any more damage.

The worst thing about something like this was this ole boy could get tired of setting fires or move on into another community, and they might never catch him. Times like this, he saw a good reason for bounty hunters like Rose. She had few restrictions other than obey the law of the place she was at.

He chuckled under his breath. Bounty hunters often stretched the law as tight as possible, and there were good ones and bad. Right now, he'd give anything to look up and see Rosie Parsons fully armed and standing between him and these dang dumb yahoos. But most times a fella had to make his own getaway, especially when he walked into it on purpose.

SIX

IF ANY PLACE WAS BARREN, it was the panhandle of Texas. And, boy, was it hot, too. If she was burning up and worn out, then poor Cimarron must be roasting. Rose dismounted and led the patient animal. Ahead, the sun swallowed up the horizon. Then, right there, where she could reach out and touch it, was a sagging sign. *Hawkins Post.* She'd been here before but, blinded by the sun, didn't recognize the small place.

It was one of those little-known places named, as many were, after the first family to settle there. Having been here before she knew a bit of its history. The entire family had been slaughtered in the Red River Wars in 1874, and a single grave marked by a large stone was all that remained to remind those who lived here and those who passed through. Folks who knew the place speculated where the stone had come from considering the surrounding bare countryside.

To learn more anyone could provide whiskey and some curiosity to an elderly man by the name of August and sit beside him near the stagecoach line that passed through on the way from Amarillo to Santa Fe. A log stage stop to feed and rest riders, it contained a good-sized corral to house spare horses. The settlement wasn't far from the river that served the area with water, feed and rest for men and beasts. Everything located there was either in the stage stop or the post.

Marshal Julio Jenkins, Apache on his mother's side and mostly white on his father's, had a desk in one corner of the large log building. He kept the peace in the entire county with the help of his younger cousin, Angelo, a full-blood Apache and as strong as an oak tree. He was all the help Marshal Jenkins ever needed. Both must've changed their names from Running Horse or Standing Bear or something like that, obviously to match the majority of brown skinned residents.

Rose had been here before and learned the history from August the first time. Today she was in Hawkins to speak to Marshal Jenkins. Tying Cimarron at the hitching rail, she stomped dust from her boots and brushed at her britches before going in and heading straight for the marshal's desk in the shadowy corner of the post. A tall man with a mustache to be proud of sat behind the desk going through a stack of wanted posters. Marshal Jenkins himself. He glanced up when she approached.

He didn't smile but greeted her civilly. "Rose, good to see you."

"Same to you, Marshal." She didn't like him either.

"How's business? Making any money killing folks?"

Hard to get information during a fight, so she ignored the cutting tone. "Actually, I'm hoping to save some lives. I'm looking to find out the names of the posse who burned out that fellow a few months back. I understand he's on a wanted poster with a substantial reward."

"Why would a bounty hunter want to save lives? Especially of a posse? I understand your interest in the reward."

"You think it gives me pleasure to see those families being burned up?"

"Anyone who hunts and kills for money has no sympathy."

His people had a reputation for killing, but she kept her mouth shut about that. "I think it might be him who is responsible for the fires at ranches in the area in the past few months. All I'd like is to talk to the posse members, see if some of them have been burned out and warn the rest of them."

"What you are seeking is to carry him in for the bounty, or worse, cut off his head. I know your practices." He pursed his lips, studied one of the wanted posters as if dismissing her. Finally, he slanted his eyes in her direction. "I am trying to understand what your true reason for wanting this information could be. What is it you whites say? Ulterior motive?"

"Why play Indian, Julio? You know that I know you graduated from a white college back east. I'm trying to stop this brutality. Burning ranches with families in them isn't something either you nor I condone. So, let's stop this game. If you know some names tell me, or at least warn them that I believe he's doing this to avenge his own family's death."

He stared at her. "I'm not real fond of bounty hunters. You shoot and ask questions later. Now you want to go after a man who lost his wife and baby? Want to send others after him too? Get out of my town before I arrest you."

She didn't mind much lying to get what was justice, so she stared him down. "I'm not after the man, have no interest." She'd gladly call the man out and shoot him, but not the kid.

He half rose from the chair, palming his six-shooter. "Leave now. Go somewhere else with your lies, or I will find a reason to lock you up. I would bet you got some illegal killings in your past."

She held up both palms. "Okay, I'm leaving. But when he keeps up these killings, something will have to be done, and it'll be another posse. And you can bet your bottom dollar there'll be a price on his head. They'll hang him, so you might reconsider."

Furious, she stomped across the large room, her boots thudding on the wooden floor, while customers buying or trading for supplies watched in silence.

Outside on the boardwalk, she studied the few people in the small settlement. No man with a young boy looked suspicious. She'd almost slipped to the sheriff that there might be two outlaws running together, one a young kid she didn't want hurt. Let the old fart find out for himself. She had wanted posters on both, and could earn perhaps five thousand dollars when she brought them both in. Dead or Alive was printed on the bottom of both. Sometimes she wondered at the way the law worked.

The more she thought about Jenkins' attitude the madder she got. Anger filled her with a near explosive rage, but she knew better than to blow up at a marshal, even if he wasn't federal, but just a town lawman. He was looking for an excuse to put her in jail. Time for her to get out of this place and contact Dell Hoffman. At least he didn't think she went around shooting people just for the money. He knew better, and she was going to need help to put this to rest without more innocent deaths.

A sign at the stage stop said a telegraph office was located there. She crossed the main dirt road that fronted the post and hurried inside the stage stop. She sure wasn't afraid of Julio Jenkins but didn't want to be involved in a gunfight in the middle of his place either.

At the counter she dictated the wire.

```
Lots to tell you STOP Meet me in Cactus Junction
soonest STOP Rose
```

It was near dark when she stepped outside. Time to set up a camp and try to figure out her next move. While waiting for Sheriff Hoffman she might talk to August after all. Julio Jenkins was right about one thing. Once it was proven who the fire starter was, the bounty would grow huge, and she would be happy to collect his head and the money. And August knew about everything that went on around this part of the panhandle.

Untying Cimarron, she walked with him over to the stoop where August sat alone, waiting for the stage and someone who would stop and talk to him and offer him a few cents for any information he shared.

She dropped the weary mount's reins. Tired as he was, he would stand as long as he could see her. A log for visitors lay alongside the old man. She introduced herself and sat.

One or two questions should open him up. Before she could say more than her name, he caught her gaze with rheumy blue eyes. "You the lady bounty hunter?"

"I am, yes. How did you know about me?"

He smiled, revealing ragged, black teeth. "August knows about everyone. It is his job."

"Good, because I need to know about someone and hope you'll share what you know with me."

He held out a hand, brown skin wrinkled over gnarly knuckles. The smile remained in place.

She pulled the small bag from between her breasts, opened it and took four bits out. "Is this enough?"

He closed his fingers over the coins. "That will depend on who you want to know about. Some I cannot share, some cost more to share, and maybe a few are not worth even what they believe they might be worth. So, we shall see."

This could cost her more than it was worth. Might as well try, though. "I would like to learn the name of the one who is burning the ranches." He probably didn't know, but it was worth trying first.

He looked far away. Scratched his chin with yellowed nails. "Many are burned out now."

"Yes, but I wish to know who is doing this terrible thing."

"Ah, you remember I said some cost the most?"

She was afraid of that. "Yes, how much to tell me his name and the names of those he still wants to burn. The other posse members?"

"More than you might have in your little bag. You already know more than most."

So, she was right about this.

Her heart skittered around. Would he know the names of the posse members, too? The little bag only carried money for incidentals. The money she made on bounty was kept in a secret place and she had no wish to reveal it here. But if he knew all the posse riders who might be victims of the fire starter she would. Mouth dry with anticipation, she looked him in the eyes. "So, tell me how much."

"This you gave me plus this many times." He held up five fingers. "That is a lot, but he is a bad man and August does not wish to die by him."

"That would only happen if I told him where I got my information. And I will not tell him."

"I do not know that."

"What will make you know that?"

He smiled his snaggle-toothed smile once more and held up five fingers, took them down, then up again.

"And the names of the posse?"

He frowned, and it looked like clouds had come over his features. "No, there is not enough for that." He closed his hand into a fist. "August does not wish to talk with you about this. You ask too much."

The old fart probably didn't know. Or maybe he didn't care what happened to the others.

So, ten times four bits. "Put out your hand for the fire starter's name."

He shook his head. "You go away now. Do not come back and ask August anything."

She turned the bag upside down and dumped all the coins into her hand. "You may have all these if you give me the fire starter's name."

He stared at the pile of coins. Maybe, five or six dollars' worth. "You will not cheat August?"

"Of course not. As long as you tell me the truth."

"His name is truly Amos Horner, but that is not the name he is using now. That I cannot tell you." He pointed toward his palm. "I will not tell you the others. They will get what they deserve."

She emptied the coins into his hand. "Thank you."

He nodded. "Do not go too close to this man, or he will kill you."

"I'll remember that. I have to go now."

The dirty old man thought what he said was true and that's why he gave her Horner's name. He wanted him to kill her. Well, that wouldn't happen.

Picking up Cimarron's reins, she climbed up in the saddle. It had been a long day, and all she wanted was to lie down somewhere, but not here so close to Hawkins Post. Too many people. Perhaps, in the morning she would be able to pick up the trail of the lightning bolt once more. What if she continued to follow it and then it wasn't who she was after? The posters had the name of Amos Horner for escaping, and she'd heard he had been burned out by the posse. August truly believed he was also the fire starter, but there was no bounty on him for that, only for suspicion which meant he had to be taken in alive.

Hoffman believed there soon would be a bounty on him for the arsons too, but someone would have to prove he was the arsonist and, so far, that hadn't happened. When and if it did, that bounty would soar. To ask him to meet her at the remote junction where the road to Santa Fe crossed the one to Amarillo made sense. No matter where Sheriff Hoffman was in the panhandle, he would be about the same distance from Cactus Junction.

Quite a place, Cactus Junction. Situated square dab in the center of the Panhandle, it attracted a mixture of humanity. The state itself might have a wild reputation, but it was nothing compared to this gathering of saloons and churches, all at odds with each other.

She arrived on a beautiful Sunday morning, reluctantly surrendered her Colt and rifle to a deputy at the U.S. marshal's office and rode leisurely through town surrounded by wagons filled with folks in their Sunday-go-to-meeting clothes. She felt naked without her weapons. Didn't matter that people were laughing and shouting, and there was no gunplay or violence.

Looked like, on a Sunday, wagons from all directions descended on the place to attend one of the churches. The Mexicans celebrated Mass at Our Lady of Guadalupe, the Whites preferred the Methodist or the Baptist, and the Indians were well mixed in all three plus holding their own religious rites on top of a rise overlooking town—the latter not necessarily on Sunday.

She rode past brilliantly painted saloons that took up a good deal of two sides of the main street. Unlike other businesses, all were open. Inside, noisy, chattering, laughing people carried on their own particular kind of worship. They played cards, rolled dice, bet on a wheel and gambled in every way known to man. Not many people lived in the settlement itself. Mostly ladies of the night with their cribs well established and those who owned the various businesses who made their living there. It was where people from all over the county went to let off steam, and so there were eight well-armed deputies plus a U.S. marshal making it one of his regular stops, and his two deputies on site, all paid out of the coffers of the gambling businesses.

It was told you could stand on a street corner there and sooner or later see most everyone who lived in west Texas, and parts of New Mexico and Colorado. Thus, it followed that at least a few of the members of the particular posse in question would sooner or later pay a visit there. She and Hoffman could find out pretty quick if any of them had been the victim of an arsonist and prove her theory. Identifying the remainder would prove more difficult, but it could then be possible to set a trap for the arsonist at one of their ranches that hadn't yet been burnt.

Only one problem. Folks didn't trust a bounty hunter like her, thus a need for Dell Hoffman, a well-known and trusted sheriff out here in west Texas. No way could she handle a posse of men on her own, so she'd wait for Hoffman. She rode directly to the wagon camp on the north side of town. The camp made it easy for gamblers to ride in and stay a while in some comfort. They could sleep in their wagons and enjoy whatever the town had to offer in entertainment. Those who didn't have a wagon were put up in a barn-like building and their animals corralled on the opposite side. It was an idea she expected might catch on in towns like Deadwood and Wichita.

She left Cimarron in a comfortable stall and paid for her own bed too, then strolled down the street. The sheer enjoyment of the people in town sent a chill of excitement through her. The gatherings where some danced were set apart from those who visited or shared food. Church goers came out in groups and strolled through town, some taking part in the frivolities including gambling.

Someone shouted behind her, and she turned and came face to face with Rafe Malone, the man she'd shot and sent to prison years ago. Her heart stilled, and the smile on her face froze. Seven years ago. Dear God, she should've killed him when she had the chance.

DELL DIDN'T CONSIDER HIMSELF AT the beck and call of the bounty

hunter he fondly called Rosie, yet he had found her instincts trustworthy. Besides, he was only about a short day's ride from Cactus Junction when he stopped at a railroad depot to send a wire only to be caught by hers. Sometimes they thought alike, and he often wondered where she'd learned her skills. Cactus Junction might just be where they could cast out a net and learn something about this wicked murdering fire starter. He was about to give up on the man ever leaving a clue that would lead the law to him. He was wily as a fox, mean as a she-bear with cubs, and had never been seen carrying out his dirty deed.

So, he rode into the town with at least a plan. Find Texas Rose Parsons and see what she had to say for herself, then get this done so he could get back home. He sure did miss Guinn, and the sooner they settled this business, the sooner he could get back to her. In fact, if Texas got much wilder, he was taking her and all their belongings and settling in Colorado where there was mostly peace and quiet.

Curly walked unperturbed down the crowded street. Not a spooky horse, he usually calmed even the most distressed. That included Dell and his pack horse. He read off the names of the saloons as he rode past trying to figure where Rosie might be. Right ahead so he couldn't miss it was a painted sign with a yellow rose on it. Of course, where else?

Tying his horse out front, he whispered in his ear, "You take care of things out here, now." The animal nodded as if he understood, and Dell figured he did...when he wanted.

As he climbed the steps to the boardwalk in front of the Yellow Rose, a cowboy came flying through the door, his hat sailing behind. "And don't come back, cheater," an angry voice behind him said.

Several passers-by stopped to laugh, but Dell slipped right on through the doors. A man yelled, "Atta girl, Shirley, you show 'em."

Everyone inside was flat-out having too much fun for a man as peaceful as Dell, so he ignored the noisy frivolity and scanned each face 'til he spotted Rosie in her familiar red blouse, blue britches, and black Stetson barely covering her mane of streaked hair. He must've been obvious, too, 'cause she raised a hand and hollered something which he took to be his name. Fighting his way through the happiest crowd he'd seen in ages, he reached her just as some fella came up behind her and pinched her. Dell stopped dead still, moved out of the guy's forward path, and puckered his mouth.

Man hadn't ought to've done that.

She swung around with one arm extended and caught the offender smack on the jaw with a fist. He went down amidst the many legs and feet, and they all let him lie. Just stumbled around and over him. Rosie gestured to Dell and headed for the back where a door let them out in the dark, silent night away from the noise.

"Break your hand?" He laughed with her.

"Nah, but it hurt. Was worth it. What is it with men and pinching women's butts?"

"Well, guess I'd better not try to answer that one. How you been?"

"Perplexed. I did find out from August over in Hawkins Post that Amos Horner is the one starting the fires for sure."

"Now, if only we could get him in court to swear to it."

"He wouldn't open up about the posse members, though, but he knows who they are."

"Old man knows everything. Wouldn't talk, huh?"

"Nope. Gave him all the coin I had just for Horner's name."

For a while, neither said anything. They stood under the stars in silence. He finally spoke. "What do you want?"

She cocked her head, as if his tone puzzled her, but it shouldn't. They both knew many things are not spoken. What he knew about her, and she knew about him.

"I think we can find this killer, but I can't do it on my own. Too many people don't trust me."

He grinned, knowing she could only see the gleam of his eyes in the dark. "What you get for being on the wrong side of the law."

"Come on, let's walk before someone decides to look for us. Earning bounty for catching outlaws isn't exactly on the wrong side of the law."

"I know, but a lot of folks don't. Now, what's going on?"

She told him her theory as briefly as possible. He listened closely because she was a smart woman, and he trusted her judgment. When she finished, they had walked to the end of the string of saloons and crossed over to continue on the other side in the shadows.

"Sounds plausible, but how are we going to fix it?" He took her elbow down the boardwalk steps and past a crossroad.

"You're the law. We need the names of the men in the posse that burned him out. They are the victims. Much as I hate to say it, he's the killer, he and his son both are probably setting the fires. Truth be known, I can't say as I blame him for his rage, but I can't condone his solving of the pain he feels. He's only making matters worse."

"You know Rosie, that we can't start at the backend of this. First, we have to learn if we're right before we start assigning victims or killers to this sick business."

"I know. Get the names of the posse so we can find out if it's only their ranches that have been burned. That's a start."

"I'll try to do it right and proper and talk to the deputies or the sheriff.

The marshal's not in town. If they don't know, I may have to contact him for more information, then let you know. If everything isn't handled right a posse often just forms up and later no one is sure who they rode with. We'll see what we see. Where you staying?"

"I'm going to bed down at the wagon camp. Me and Cimarron."

"You be careful. There's some pretty rough *hombres* sleeping off their drunks there."

"I'm a big girl. I can handle any drunk."

"Oh, I know—and you're mean, too. Stay that way." Her laughter rang to the thudding of his boot heels on the wooden walk.

Trail weary but not ready to bed down, Dell hooked a turn into the first saloon he came to after he left Rosie. Not really much of a drinker or gambler, he still liked to wet his whistle occasionally. Besides, he might hear something helpful where people gathered. So, he worked his way past elbows and bodies 'til he arrived at the bar. The place was busy, but the bartender was on the ball, and when he caught the eye of a newcomer, he took his order.

"I'll have a brew." Dell twirled a two-bit piece on the counter. The fellow behind the bar quickly slapped it and dragged it under his palm. "You know when the marshal's coming back?" He moved the lapel of his jacket just enough so the kid saw the badge on his chest.

"Heard he's gone off into New Mexico. They got a range war going on. May be a spell. We have us a town marshal and sheriff and deputies." Braggadocio colored the man's voice, like he had something to do with the good law enforcement in town. "One of them might could help you."

The beer appeared before him, and he took a long sip. Cold. They were hauling in ice by rail. Lots of money being made in this town.

He thanked the bartender and turned sideways to check out the crowd, hoping for a familiar face. He got around pretty good, didn't see anyone offhand. First thing in the morning, he'd go visit with the local marshal and the sheriff. He'd learn something yet, by god.

SEVEN

ROSE SNUGGLED INTO HER BEDROLL spread in the hay barn, sleep
evading her. The long day's ride should have worn her out, but here she
lay wide awake. The smell of fresh-cut hay reminded her of her childhood,
playing in the barn before her grandparents died and she and Mama had to
move to town and start Dottie Lou's. Everything changed then, for both of
them. Life was never the same.

Perhaps it was catching sight of Rafe that kept her awake. Every time
she closed her eyes, she saw that monster, her first bounty capture. Taken
alive. How long ago now? Five years, six? Who kept track of that? Yet she
couldn't forget the hatred in his eyes when she shot the gun from his hand,
the way he stared at her in the courtroom when she testified against him
for the brutal beating of his mother and his wife. Both had survived, but
they were changed forever. Now, he was out of prison and back in Texas.
She might have to kill him this time. 'Cause he would not have stopped
showing brutality to women.

She should've told Hoffman about seeing him, but if she had, then he'd
have been more concerned about her than this job. And they had to catch
this guy without getting hurt. Both of them. The thought of more people

burned alive at the hands of this killer terrified her. Far as she knew only one family had gotten out alive, but the father was badly burned rescuing his children.

Scattered survivors had happened. It was a big territory, but the word of something like this got around, and there had been five ranchers burned out, two families were all dead, two had some survivors. That was outrageous. She was afraid to add up the children who had perished, but one family had four. It was too bad the names of the others in jeopardy weren't known, so they could be warned. She could only hope they had somehow heard and were taking precautions.

The sun awoke her from a nightmare she tried not to remember. Where was she? It took a few moments for her to remember that she was in Cactus Junction sleeping in the barn provided for those in town without wagons and with six bits to spare. No doubt she was the only woman here. This type of fresh hay bedding suited very few. Some of the fancier saloons offered rooms to those with plenty of money to lose at the tables.

She had slept a bit but got little rest. Searching for Sheriff Hoffman could wait 'til after breakfast. Give him time to talk to the lawmen and maybe get some names to start with. Much as she was used to riding, her body had some sore spots that a good walk would help work out. She had fried eggs, some beans and potatoes, then walked the town from one end to the other. It was enjoyable to gaze in all the windows at the finery. Mostly to make fun of it. My goodness, the frilly clothes women liked to get up in. How did they manage to do anything but sit and fan themselves to keep cool? For a while she could forget seeing Rafe, concentrate on finding the sheriff while mocking the bustles and low-cut gowns that lifted their ample boobs under their chins.

Enough of this nonsense. Look for the sheriff's tall straight figure. It would stand out in the crowd. He might be with one of the lawmen, so she drifted toward Sheriff Franklin Boyd's office. Because of the hard feelings between her and the law she casually peered in as she walked by. Didn't see him, then headed for the town marshal, Eben Hunter's. He wasn't there either. A deputy glanced out the window, and she scurried to get out of sight.

Too late, he burst through the door and caught her arm with a big hand. "Looking for someone, ma'am?"

"Just taking a stroll. Let go."

He jerked her around and shoved her inside before she could resist. "Just step this way. We need to have a talk."

She ought to set her feet and fight back, but maybe she'd better not. The law liked to throw her behind bars just to show they could. She didn't resist when he pushed her down in a chair at the desk inside.

"Where's your marshal? I'd like to speak to him."

"He's not here right now. What does a bounty hunter want with the marshal, anyway?"

She tilted her head and smiled like she'd learned years ago when Mama taught her to control men. "Just wanted to say hello."

"Oh, sure." He sat behind the desk, opened the drawer and took out a ring of keys. Jangled them in her sight. "Jail cell keys. I'm going to search you for a weapon. You know they're not allowed within the city limits."

"I don't have a weapon, but you put your hands on me again, and you'll pull back a stub."

He rose and kicked back the chair. "Threatening a deputy. That calls for some time behind those bars. You should've behaved yourself and stayed in the kitchen cooking for your man."

"I don't have a man, nor want one. If you wonder why, look at yourself in the mirror, or think of the way you're acting."

Someone opened the door and stepped inside. The deputy raised his eyes. "Marshal, I was just—"

"I know what you were just, *deputy.*" He placed a special emphasis on the title. "I'll handle this. Ma'am. Miz Parsons, isn't it? I'm so sorry I'm late. I ran across Sheriff Hoffman a moment ago, and he told me you were in town and he was looking for you. He's just down at the Yellow Rose waiting for you. I told him I could probably find you." Eben Hunter smiled cordially and escorted her out the door, closing it behind her.

How odd. She hadn't time to utter a sound. Shaking her head, she hurried along the boardwalk her attention on finding the sign for the Yellow Rose. Funny, that's how she'd been known in Fort Smith at Dottie Lou's. Some people still called her that, though she'd been out of the business for several years.

Not paying attention to her own safety, it was too late when she stepped down off the boardwalk at the cross street, and arms grabbed her roughly. The dragged her into the shadows. A gloved hand covered her mouth, and words were spat wetly in her ear.

"Stop fighting or I'll slit yer purty throat. And that there's a plumb purty sight. Yum."

Brain screaming in terror, she kicked and flailed in silence. Rafe was seeking his revenge, and he would kill her.

Saying nothing else he continued to drag her further and further from the main street into a narrow area cluttered with busted crates, broken wheels off wagons, piles of rags. When fighting only made him treat her rougher she went totally limp, hoping to make it harder for him to handle her. She was a big gal, almost six feet and well-muscled so she carried a good weight. If he were to let up on her for even a minute, she'd do some damage to him. Whether she got away or not was iffy, but she could hurt him. Yet he kept a tight grip, even when he lashed her wrists behind her back and crooked an arm around her neck to drag her backwards.

As long as her feet were on the ground, she had a chance, but once he bundled her up into a wagon or lashed her stomach-down on a horse, she had little chance of escaping. How could she have been so careless? Had to be Rafe. Surely, no one else would dare do this. His arm around up upper body squeezed so tight she could barely breathe, and she gasped for air.

Then what she'd feared happened. He tossed her in the back of a wagon where someone else lay across her while he tied her ankles. She managed to shout once before a rag was stuffed in her mouth. Despite all her struggles they had her trussed up with a sack over her eyes in jig-time. So, it took at least two to accomplish this. Rafe and a friend?

In a town like Cactus Junction no one would've paid attention to one short shout, so she ceased her struggles. No point in wearing herself out. A chance to escape would come, and she'd be ready.

The wagon sagged to one side and started to move with her captor beside her. The two arsonists? Or someone else she'd put in jail over the years. Several bounty captures were dead and buried in the ground, but she no longer remembered them all. And the one she knew lived and was out, was Rafe Malone.

They moved slowly away from the noise of town, and she tried to keep track of how far they went. Somehow, she would get away from them. She had to think that way. As time and distance passed, even after they dragged her from the wagon, draped her over a horse's back and the animal started down, hope hung in there. There was only one place in the panhandle that trails headed down this steeply. Her heart beat faster for they were going into Palo Duro Canyon where outlaws hid—Lots of outlaws that she had seen put away over the years. Many of whom would be happy to see her dead. Dammit, how come she had to let that thought in? Some she had helped when things went bad on them, and they were either innocent or right in their choices. Remembering that right wasn't always legal. Hope was all she had.

Hoffman would search for her when he found Cimarron stabled at the wagon camp in Cactus Junction. Lawmen hated going down into Palo Duro alone. It took a posse to flush out a gang in there. But she had one hope and that was that her friends J.T. and Jake Harper were still camped out there. They might hear of her plight. She never took out after them, and they knew why. Like her, they believed that justice was more important than a bad law, and they weren't always the same. They stuck to that doctrine and knew she did, too.

Her captors said very little on the rough ride down. Surprisingly, the animal she was on was sure-footed, but his hooves still skidded once in a while. They must've put her on a sure-footed mule. No one would trust a horse and rider making it safely to the bottom of the canyon unless they were blamed fools. Best she couldn't see, but which was worse? Imagining a fall or having one? Her only relief was the removal of the rag from her mouth. Even if she yelled, no one would hear her. The bouncing while tied stomach down put her in agony before they reached the bottom.

Someone hollered. "Hey, you're late."

Her hair was yanked. "See you got her. Give you any trouble?"

"Nah, let's get her on back to the camp 'fore someone comes along."

Laughter. "Who the hell would care? Everyone down here'd be happy to see her all trussed up like that, wouldn't they?"

"Yeah, we might ought to parade her around for a bit, let everyone take a lick at her."

"Well, not *quite* everyone."

There, that one. She knew his voice. Maybe.

Or maybe it was just her imagination.

The ride began once more, but at least they were in the bottom. Still, it was no picnic. Her stomach roiled. Again, a rag stuffed in her mouth, she could suffocate if she vomited. She swallowed several times and tried to think of pretty things. But all she could picture was these toughs were going to have some fun with her then kill her, so she had to grab the first chance she got to get away, no matter how dangerous.

At last, the animal stopped, and someone dragged her off. Her chin landed painfully in a rocky patch of ground, and when they rolled her over, hot blood trickled along her jawline.

"Take that rag out her mouth 'fore she chokes." A different and definitely familiar voice. One she'd heard recently right here in this canyon. Someone with the Jake Harper gang? Surely not. Jake would have their hide.

"Why? What difference do it make if she dies now or later?"

A loud spat. "Fool. We got her. We can have some fun with her first. Didn't go to all that trouble back in town to not play a while later."

She gagged, couldn't hold it back any longer. Noises rose from down in her throat. If they didn't do something she would pass out. They were all laughing too hard to care, and she spun from panic into darkness.

WHEN ROSIE FAILED TO SHOW up at the saloon where Dell waited, he stomped all over the crazy town one more time without finding a trace of her. Marshal Franklin assured him that he'd sent her down to the Yellow Rose when she dropped by. Time to face that something had happened to her. Something bad. Now he'd have to deal with some smart-mouthed deputies who liked to give bounty hunters like her a hard time. Most couldn't face the idea that without the help of hunters like her, too many bad men would ride free. There weren't enough of them to keep the bad ones down. It wasn't like she took anything away from them but maybe their reputation.

He marched up the steps to the town marshal's office. He'd only met Marshal Hunter a couple of times. Competent, young, and a bit of a smart-ass. As good a place to start as any, and he was more than ready for him to smart off when Rose's name came up. A young deputy came out of the back room looking a little the worse for wear. He glanced at Dell and fingered his mussed hair back.

"Help you, sir?"

Dell flipped up his lapel. "Dell Hoffman, Sheriff out of Saddler County. Looking for Rose Parsons. She was going to meet me today on a matter of some importance, and she seems to have disappeared. Seen her?"

The kid rocked back on his heels. "Don't reckon. Doesn't ring any bells."

"She's a bounty hunter out of Legend County, looking to find this arsonist that's been plaguing everyone."

The kid snorted. "You working with a bounty hunter, and a woman at that? Sinking pretty blamed low, ain't you?"

"Look, I'm not asking for your opinion on my character since you're not qualified along that line. Seen her or not?"

"Don't recall being formally introduced to anyone with that name. What's she look like?"

"You could be hindering the capture of a dangerous criminal. And if you are, I'll be back, and you'll be the one in jail."

"I'll see you then, and maybe she'll be in there with me."

"When hell freezes over and it rains toad frogs. Fool."

Before knocking his shoulders up around his ears, Dell left and headed for the sheriff's office. He'd known Sheriff Franklin Boyd a while, and he was older, had a bit better sense than that crazy marshal. Sometimes city marshals got a bit stuck on themselves. Especially the younger ones without as much law experience. Sometimes it was difficult to find men to fill law jobs in Texas. It was too big and too wild with range wars and ranchers thinking they were the law when they owned thousands of acres of land. Some of those ranchers had entire towns in their grasp. Surely, Sheriff Boyd would have better sense than that yahoo.

Too bad, but Boyd hadn't heard a word about the arsonist problems. "Say, Hoffman, if you had to try to keep this wild-ass town toeing the line, you wouldn't know much of what goes on outside its city limits either. If I ain't corralling a bunch of wild cowboys riding their hosses right into one saloon or another, I'm pulling them apart from fist fights. The gambling here attracts every cowpoke, outlaw and worthless bum you can imagine. So, I'm afraid I can't help you much with this fire starter. Who'd ever think someone would go on a rampage like that? I don't know what this world is coming to.

"You're looking for a bounty hunter you say? You crazy or what?"

Though he was beginning to feel a bit crazy, he sure as hell was sorry he'd even brought up the subject. The man paced the whole time he ranted and liked to never wound down. When he did, Dell didn't want to ask him another question.

It appeared the lawmen in this town had so many of their own problems they'd not heard a whole lot about the ranches being burned up in Saddler and Legend County.

"Right now," the sheriff went on, "I've got two deputies out running down a couple yahoos who robbed the Black Jack Table over at The Golden Mule, another I just sent to break up a fight at The Sand Dollar, and I need someone to go with me to find out who stole a wagon and a mule and maybe kidnapped a woman. Anyways, someone going by the alleyway heard her screaming, saw her kicking."

Only half-listening, Dell broke in there. "Can you tell me what alleyway? I'll look into it myself if you don't care. Maybe take a good look around town see what I can find out. Sorry for your troubles."

Grumbling to himself, Dell stomped into the street where he now stood hands on his hips contemplating saloons ever which way he looked. All filled with folks not minding giving their money away. No one could take notice of much else. So, he'd start where she'd stayed the previous night and go from there. Rosie liked a good drink, so one of the many drinking places would be next in line.

At the wagon camp, he went in search of someone in charge of overnight guests. Inside the large barn, horse stalls lined one long side while beds were set up in private sleeping areas. Looking for a human, he was surprised to hear a horse pawing and snorting as if to get his attention. He finally headed for the stalls to find Cimarron, head hanging far out a stall. He'd spotted Dell and kicked up a fuss.

"Well, look. You lonely? Where's our Rosie?" He rubbed the soft nose.

"Hey, mister. Looking for someone?" A bowlegged cowboy thin as a plank sidled his way.

"Yeah, where's the woman who owns this horse?"

"I reckon I'm not sure, but she lit out walking this morning. Going for breakfast. Never come back. Not too unusual. Prob'ly at one of them gaming tables. Easy to get caught up in them. Air she in trouble?"

Dell showed his badge. "A friend of mine. We were supposed to meet this morning."

"Well, that's all I can tell you, Sheriff. Sorry. If you want, you kin ask around. Folks in and out all day in wagons and the like."

"Appreciate it, sir. I'll do that if it's no problem."

"None I can think of. Course there might be some folk who'd take a potshot at the law, so take care."

"Found it odd everyone carries their gun in this town."

"Oh, heck yeah. All afraid they'll get shot if they don't." The cowboy doubled over with laughter. "Makes wobbledy sense, don't it?"

Dell chuckled. "Yeah, I can see where sense is the last thing in this town. I'm going to look around some more. If she does come back, would you tell her I'm over at the Yellow Rose? I'll wait there unless we find each other."

"Will do."

After talking to just about everyone he could find around the wagon camp, which wasn't very many, considering more were doing something or other, Dell started at the saloons, leaving the Yellow Rose for last since he'd already waited there earlier with no luck.

A good time later when he came out of the one right next to it, a small place called the Jingling Spur, clouds had gathered, the wind was up, and jags of lightning sliced great chunks out of the grey sky. In the distance, strikes hit the ground, sometimes two or three in a row. His ears popped. The air reeked of ozone. The hair on his arms stood. A typical Texas storm. A sudden rain caught him so quick he was soaked time he ducked into the swinging doors of his objective. Checking out even the darkest of corners yielded no Rosie. Mind astir with worry he parked at the bar, rested a boot on the foot rail and ordered a beer.

Like all the saloons he'd been in it was a busy place and it took some time to get the attention of the bartender long enough to ask his questions.

A mostly bald fellow with an apron tied around his good-sized middle took the time to listen to his question and reply to his request.

He scratched a tuft of white hair behind one ear. "A woman, you say. Tall and dressed in britches? I'd remember that. What color was her hair?"

Down the way someone hollered, "Dang it, I need another brew."

"Just hold on, I'm helping the law here. You'll get your turn."

About five men bellied up at the bar, looked around and took off when they heard his words.

"Reckon you run off some customers right quick, Fred."

The fat man grinned. "Got no use for folks who break the law. Let 'em go."

The man next to Dell took a sip of beer and studied the tender behind the bar. "Plenty more where they come from, huh? I might've seen your lady in britches earlier, sheriff, but I'm not real sure."

Nearby, lightning struck with a loud clash, making everyone jump. A few women screeched.

Fred eyed him as if unperturbed. "How could you not be sure? How many ladies in britches do we see come in here?"

Dell perked right up. "When might this've been?"

"Earlier today, only she weren't in here. She was walking along the boardwalk, then some fellow stepped out, looked like he was hugging her. Say, is there a reward for this information?"

Fred banged an empty mug on the counter. "You want me to shoot you? Talk to the man."

"Hugging her? Could he have been grabbing her?"

"I reckon. Heck, I never thought of it at the time, but might be."

"Could you give me a description?"

"I was plumb across the street, but she had a mane of this gold hair."

Dell struggled to hold his temper. "What about him?"

"Uhm, not quite as tall as her, but he had on black pants with silver conchos down the sides. Like maybe he was an Indian or Mexican. Couldn't see much else from over here."

"Where did they go?"

"Back into that gap between them buildings yonder." He pointed with a dirty finger.

"Come show me."

"It's raining out there."

Fred calmly poured out the last of the man's beer on the floor and slammed down the empty mug in front of him. "You go show this man right now, or I'll see you don't get served another drop in this entire town. And believe me I can do that, too."

The man gave Fred and Dell a dirty look, then stomped out onto the boardwalk where a balcony overhead protected them from rain and pointed out the same alley the sheriff had mentioned earlier. "A wagon left soon after, but I couldn't see who was in it other than the man with silver conchos."

Dell took a two-bit piece out of his pocket and handed it to the man. "Buy yourself another beer with this, and I thank you, sir."

The man's eyes widened, and he took the money. "Thanks, Sheriff."

Head down and holding his hat on, Dell splatted across the street, fast getting wet and, muddy, and sloshed into the alley. Thankfully, it was protected by an overhang for an outside entrance to an upstairs. The ground was only slightly damp and had held prints well. He hunkered down and checked out the wagon ruts and horses' hoof prints and noted a strange jagged mark in one of the horseshoes. Looked like a lightning strike, but that wouldn't help him much 'cause it wouldn't be long before the prints were gone if this rain kept up. He studied a tore up patch of dirt that looked like someone had had a fight. If they took Rose, it wouldn't have been easy. Rubbing a boot toe in the soil he unearthed a silver concho, polished the dirt off it and stuck it in his pocket. At the corner of the building, out from under the overhanging balcony the fast disappearing wagon wheel prints headed across the Santa Fe Road to the southwest.

"Oh, Rosie... what've you gone and done now?"

EIGHT

IT'D BEEN A LONG TIME since Rose had let something so dangerous happen to her. How could she have been so foolish as to go flitting down the street like a silly goose paying little attention to what was going on around her? It didn't feel like it, but she'd got exactly what she deserved. Dad gum, she hoped she didn't pay the ultimate price for it. Best idea was to stop feeling sorry for herself and figure a way out of this mess she was in. They'd tied her hands behind her, bound her ankles with rope, propped her against a tree and left her that way for a long while, then someone came along and took the bag off her head and yanked the rag out of her mouth.

Good thing, too, she was all out of breath and gagging constantly. Her nose had stuffed up from crying, and it wouldn't be long before she passed out. Didn't help much as far as figuring out where she was. 'Cause, by then, it was right next to full dark outside, so she couldn't make out her surroundings other than a few shifting shadows that leapt around in the flashing firelight. Tied like she was, her arms and legs were asleep and useless.

Somehow, she needed to get them to untie her so she could figure a way to make them work again. The way it was she'd never be able to walk or run away. Of course, that was what they wanted. Whatever they intended to do to her they were in no big hurry.

After everyone ate sitting around the campfire—everyone but her—most settled down. Some men and women got together on their blankets on the ground having themselves a good time. Dammit, she had to start something to get out of this fix. Nearby, a young man sat against a tree whittling and occasionally glancing her way.

She leaned toward him 'til she almost fell over. "I'm hungry." First with a whisper, then she spoke a bit louder. "I need some water. Please."

He finally glanced at her sideways but kept whittling.

She tried again. "I'd be really grateful if you could get me a drink and a piece of that cornbread."

Sinking down into his shoulders he acted like he hadn't heard her.

She gave a great big sigh. "Or just a drink." Waited a bit while he formed the nose of an animal on his piece of wood. "Do you have a sister or a mother?"

He nodded but kept on with the knife.

"Would you like it if someone made them go hungry or thirsty when there was something to eat right within reach?"

"Hush up." He nearly hissed the words.

"What if I die? I haven't had a drink all day. Could you at least get me some water? I'd be so grateful." Then she took a big chance. "Some of them are going to pass me around when everyone else goes to sleep, taking turns doing you know what. I would be real good to you if you got me some water. I would say you could go first."

Without looking at her he lay down his knife and wooden animal, crawled the two steps to where the cornbread sat and, with a quick look around, grabbed it. Held it to his mouth like he might be eating it. Scooting closer he tossed it at her.

"You'll have to hold it for me or untie my hands."

The sound he made might've been a curse, she couldn't tell. But he slid on his butt 'til he was close enough to push it against her mouth. "Here, eat it, and you'd best keep your word, or I'll use that knife on your tender sweet parts. You got me?"

Nodding, she chewed and swallowed the dry cornbread as best she could 'til it began to choke her. Coughing she turned her head away. "Water. Please."

"I ain't—" He shouted without meaning to and looked all around, but no one seemed to notice. "Okay, but soon as I give you water, you gonna take care of me, like you promised. I'm needing it now, you got me all fired up."

"I will, I promise. Anything you want. Maybe when they aren't looking."

That really got him moving. He skittered along like a crab staying low 'til he found a canteen in the open and brought it back. Held it to her mouth. She gulped the warm liquid 'til she could hold no more, then turned her head away. Now would come the hard part, but she was ready. It might be her only chance. Men drinking and talking around the campfire and those on their blankets would soon decide to carry out their desires with her. She was ready to die to keep them from it if she had to. They'd left the kid to keep an eye on her and trusted he was doing it. Not paying him any attention 'cause they were all getting courage from a bottle and bragging about what they would do with her when it was their turn.

He put down the canteen and laid a hand on her thigh. She let him leave it there and wiggled seductively. "It'd be much more fun for you if I could move my legs. You could touch more."

His hands trembled and he looked all around, then back at her. She arched a bit, so she was touching him hard. He made a sound down in his throat.

Someone at the campfire hollered so loud the kid jumped like he'd been shot. He hunkered far away from her for a while 'til things quieted down over there, then crawled back like some sort of scared animal.

He sure did want what she had real bad. She would have her way, and he wasn't getting anything but a lump on the noggin. A gust of wind went through the trees, shaking a load of water down off the leaves. The kid was still so nervous he cried out and brushed at his wet hair like maybe he'd been attacked.

He must've really got his courage up, or his need got to hurting 'cause he growled down in his throat and scurried right up against her, hands all over the place. Feeling her.

"Stop. Untie me and you can do anything you want."

"Huh-uh. You'll run off soon as I do that."

She shook her head. "No, I won't. I promise. I want you. I like you better than them, they're all ugly old men with beards and black teeth. You're pretty and clean."

He reached for the front of her blouse.

"Oh, please just untie my arms so I can touch you. I want to so bad."

He shook his head fiercely, ran his fingers over the bare skin of her neck. Tried to push himself tighter against her 'til she could feel he was bad off with the wanting. Okay, he was getting ready.

"It feels good, doesn't it? Under my clothes all my skin feels like that. I'll help you, do things for you, but you'll have to untie my arms. I can't run away with my legs tied." She leaned forward 'til her mouth was on his jaw and licked him. She shuddered from the gritty feel and filthy taste. She wanted to bite his ear off and spit it at him.

"You liked that. I felt you did."

Fiercely he nodded and licked her back.

How nasty. Just a bit more. "Nice. You know if you're going to have me, you'd better hurry, they look like they're fixing to come on over here, and they won't let a kid like you near me."

"Oh shit, oh shit."

He was as ready as she could allow.

"Come on, hurry. They're coming."

He was so wrought up he didn't bother to look and see if they were or not. He shoved her over onto her belly and untied the ropes around her wrists. Fingers dug and nails picked at the damp rope. He cursed under his breath. Rubbed against her all the time. If he weren't careful, he'd get his satisfaction before he got her loose.

She did not want that. "Take it easy, it's about to come untied. Everything's okay." She inched a bit away, so he wasn't against her.

It seemed to take forever, and she wanted to scream in her need to be loose from these awful men. It was as fierce as his lust for her. Being at their mercy damaged her bad. She wasn't free yet, not quite, and she was terrified he wouldn't hurry, though he acted like it was now or never. Young men had such a harsh need for women. They needed to have it chopped off before they grew up, then they wouldn't have so many problems. Watching him doing anything just to get in her britches almost made her feel sorry for him.

All the same, she'd cut it off herself, given the chance.

Her arms came loose, but they'd been tied so long she could hardly move them. He lifted them around in front of her, gestured for her to take off the blouse or to touch him or something. He was about to panic.

"Sweetie, legs, untie my legs and I can really do what you want. Don't you see that? Come on, hurry before they see us. Maybe we should move into the bushes there, hide so we can enjoy this without them seeing."

By then it was obvious she had him. All he could think of was getting between her legs. Between working on the ropes at her ankles and trying to half drag her beneath a bunch of thick undergrowth a few feet away, he acted like he might have a stroke or bust something. Well, let him. She helped him where she could, more anxious to get loose then he was to have what he wanted.

Even when the other ropes came off, she couldn't stand. She'd crawl if she had to, but it had to be the right time. If they caught her the punishment along with them having their way would be extreme. No doubt what they had in mind, and she couldn't talk them out of it. Escape was the only answer. This had to work. He finally rolled her the last foot or so under the brush and hopped in on top of her, so ready, he could no longer see straight. Now, if only she could run or even crawl before those men telling stories and drinking came to realize what was going on.

Moving her arms around one hand came down on a rock. Her palm fit around it if only she could pick it up. With fingers like stubs, she pried it out of the wet ground. Using the heel of her hand she pushed on one side 'til the thing rolled over and under her hand. His body moved all over her, but he couldn't seem to get anywhere, though he moaned like he was enjoying himself. Maybe she ought to let him go farther, far enough to be out of his head with the pleasure.

So, keeping hold of the rock she folded herself around him, so she was enclosing him—yes—just there. And he was off, not caring about anything else. It was too late for him to remove any clothes, he just had to do this. And when he froze and made ugly sounds, she swung the rock around and caught him on the temple. If he lived through this, he might think it was the best he'd ever had. She'd felt life go out of someone once, and this was the way it felt.

Taking several deep breaths, she shoved him off like a piece of garbage, scrabbled on hands and knees out of the brush away from the campfire. She still couldn't stand, but by God she could crawl. Until she butted up against booted legs. Almost cried with disappointment.

"Well, little darlin'. Just where do you think you're going?" A gruff voice filled with delight put a stop to her escape.

ROSE WAS ON HER OWN. That was the only way Dell could look at it. Anyway, he wasn't her keeper. He didn't even know why he felt any responsibility at all for the girl.

The pouring rain continued, and he had run out of track. Just mud now, plain old mud, but he kept moving, figuring the road led back to Palo Duro, a place to start. Stir those gangs up a bit and get some information from them. Someone knew something and he wanted whoever was starting those fires, almost at any cost.

Poor Curly plodded along through rain so hard neither man nor horse could see far. The sound of another unlucky traveler approached. Dell swiped rainwater from his eyes and watched a soaked rider on a horse appear out of the distance. Just in case, he unsnapped the strap on his holster and palmed the .44 on his hip before reining in his mount.

"Howdy. Good day for a pleasure ride, ain't it?" The rider appeared to have a hand on his weapon, too.

"Not finding it too pleasurable, but sure nothing for it."

"I reckon not. " The man, a good-sized Indian from the look of it, reined up and offered a gloved hand. "John Smith."

Laughing, Dell stuck out his. "Bob Jones. Where you coming from on a day like this? We're sorta in the middle of nowhere."

"Yep, that we are. You going where I'm comin' from?"

"Looks like. Not much behind you for a ways." This was getting plumb crazy and it was time to move on. "Well, you take 'er easy and don't drown."

For a brief second he lowered his glance to retrieve the reins from around the horn. The man had a gun drawn on him when he looked back.

"Whoa. What in thunder?"

"You're under arrest, sir. Now, if you would just hand me your weapon."

Dell spurted a few choice words he kept in reserve for the worst times. "What for? I'm Sheriff Dell Hoffman out of Saddler County." He reached for his badge, bundled beneath his rain gear. The other fella had sure put a gun on him fast.

"Just hold it right there. I happen to be Marshal Jenkins from Hawkins Post and who are you? Bob Jones or Dell Hoffman? I never heard of a sheriff by the name of Jones around these parts."

"Funny, 'cause I could've sworn you said your name was John Smith, early on. Take off your hat. You look like Julio Jenkins, but in the rain it's hard to tell if you're Mister Smith or Jenkins."

The marshal holstered his gun and swept his wide-brimmed hat off.

Dell squinted at the Indian face. "I do see it's you. In all this rain gear it's sure hard to know anyone."

"And I you. I beg your pardon. Good we did not shoot each other."

"Where you headed, Marshal Jenkins?"

"Hunting down that arsonist. My deputy had a visit from a lady bounty hunter searching for the same outlaw you are. Does that not beat all? I would be glad to give you a hand. Where you are headed, you will need all the help you can get." Jenkins turned his horse away from the wind.

"Ain't that the truth. I'm heading to Palo Duro to stir up those gangs who hide out down there and see if they don't know something."

"I will turn around and join you. Let us get to riding and get down in there where we might gain some shelter from this storm before dark. There are some shelters under those bluffs."

Hard to get used to the man not using contractions, but Indians didn't tend to do so. Dell sidled his mount in beside Jenkins' horse. Not too unusual for lawmen to friend-up with an outlaw, especially one who might help him out once in a while for rewards. Almost like a bounty hunter only running with a gang. You found all kinds in Texas nowadays. If Jenkins was plumb crooked, he didn't know it. Marshals were a cut above sheriffs, so he'd lay back and see.

The farther east they rode the more the rain let up. At last, the sun peeped through a bank of clouds giving them some relief. And just in time for them to spot a roil of smoke along the horizon to the north.

Dell rose in his stirrups. Pointed. "Say, what's that look like to you?"

Julio did the same and shaded his eyes with one hand. "Not like any cloud I have ever seen. I think we should ride on over there."

The Indian was a bit slow to react until the smoke cloud poured higher. He heeled his horse into a gallop, and Dell followed suit. Curly liked to run flat out and so, obviously, did Julio's mount.

The wind in his face was damp and as clean smelling as fresh washed sheets hanging on the clothesline. Across the plains, white and yellow flowers bloomed, and this rain would bring out more to add some color to the normally brown landscape.

God, he hoped this wasn't another ranch burning. If so, maybe, it being in the early evening, everyone would be out finishing up chores before going in for supper and bedtime. He knew some of the ranches in the area but wasn't sure how far it was to the place that belonged to Herman White. He feared the fire was there.

The Apache was one hell of a rider, and his mount was a fleet-footed black stallion who ran like the wind, so he drew up a bit ahead of Dell. Throwing mud from his hooves, the horse raced into the yard between the flaming ranch house and the barn. Julio jumped off on the run, and as he did, someone raced out the side door of the larger structure, mounted a waiting horse and took off.

Go after him or help inside the house? No telling how many were inside. He cast one last glance at the fleeing fire starter. Got a good look at his horse. An Appaloosa with some peculiar markings across its butt. He vowed to remember them even as he raced the other way.

A scream lanced the air like a knife blade and Dell forgot the fleeing man to dismount on the run, stumbling to stay on his feet in the slick mud of the barnyard. Julio had disappeared in the back door of the house, and he followed him in. Be damned if he'd let him burn up in there trying to rescue someone.

Julio ran into the smoke pouring out of the bedroom where a woman screamed. Dell followed to meet the Indian carrying two children, one on each arm.

"A woman. Still in there. Could not get her."

Dell shouldered his way into the thick smoke. So thick he couldn't see. "Where are you?" He coughed on inhaling a mouthful of smoke. All he could hear now were her whimpers. "I can't see you."

"Here, over here."

He was right on top of her, but still couldn't see anything. His knees came up against a bed and he went down right on top of the woman. When he went to gather her up a baby made a weak sound. His heart filled his throat. Could he get them both? God help him and them too.

"My baby, take my baby." She was so weak he could barely hear her.

He pawed around on the bed, found the outline of her body, traced it on both sides to where she held a small bundle.

"Hold on to the babe. Hold on." His throat scratched out the words so blurred he was afraid she couldn't hear.

Gathering them both as best he could he stumbled across the room and through the main room. Fire crawled the walls and licked at his backside. The sun sent rays around the front door, and he headed that way, not sure he was going to make it. Stumbling, scrambling, he aimed for the glowing sunlight, then he burst through onto the porch, out into the yard and down on his knees, never turning loose of his precious bundle. Julio met him, took the woman and child and carried them farther away from the burning house. Dell knelt on his knees coughing. Someone put an arm around his shoulders and gave him a wet cloth.

It wasn't 'til much later that all seven survivors recovered enough to gather into the farm wagon which was parked under a big tree in the yard. The house and barn continued to burn.

Following a great deal of coughing and some crying from the woman and her children, Dell and Julio were able to find out exactly how the fire had started.

Herman White had been off in the far pasture fixing fence and was walking home when he saw the smoke. "I didn't ride out. It was just easier to walk. So, when I saw the first smoke, I ran as fast as I could, but by the time I got here you two were coming out of the house, so I ran into the barn, which he set last and got my animals out. Thank you both. You saved my entire family. I would've lost them all, I'm afraid. I couldn't have brought them all out, and her with the new babe."

He broke down crying, buried his face in his wife's bosom opposite the nursing baby.

Julio and Dell didn't get away until the entire family were taken to the ranch of a friend a few miles away and settled in. The sun set with a bloom high into the sky.

"I saw that bastard's horse, and I'll not forget it soon. Let's go on down into the canyon. We can start the search there, as we planned."

"I agree. Maybe we can find some friendlies and bed down for the night as well. That was some experience I shall not forget soon."

Dell agreed and they were soon at the cut of the canyon and a familiar trail. Julio removed his rain gear to reveal a colorful shirt decorated in hand stitchery. He was married to a full-blood Apache who must be handy with a needle. Guinn wasn't one for sewing except when she had to put on a button or sew up a rip. But she had other talents that made up for her lack. He sure wished he could finish up this hunt and get back home to her.

Jenkins started down into the canyon ahead of him, his long black hair blowing in the wind. Dell had heard Jenkins' mother was Apache, though his father was white. How could he fully trust a half-breed? Someone did, or he wouldn't be the town marshal of Hawkins Post.

"Say, marshal, did your deputy say when he talked to that woman bounty hunter?"

"Evening before last I believe." The search for Rose has slipped his mind in the excitement of the fire and its aftermath. "I sure hope she's okay, but she manages to take care of herself quite well without my help, so I think we'll stick to our search for now. We might well run across her, anyways."

"You taking to following a bounty hunter to get your outlaws?"

"Couldn't hurt if she had some idea where this evil sumbitch is."

Silence while they worked their way around a small pile of rocks likely loosened and dislodged during the rain. Dark was coming on fast, but the formations pricked the evening sky ahead.

Back on the trail, Julio snorted. "Whatever you think. She was on her way over to Cactus Junction looking for some fellas she suspicioned might be going to ground 'cause too many lawmen were on their trail." He pulled up short. "You thinking they might be hiding out in Palo Duro?"

Dell shrugged. "Where else? It's a popular hideout for the scum of the earth, and now that I've seen his horse, I'm gonna get this man 'fore he kills any more innocent families."

"Good luck. You do not even know who you are looking for."

"I'm trying to get the names of the men who were in the posse that burned him and his family out after he shot and killed that lawman. I'm thinking any one of them can be his next target and that's the way I'll get him."

"Sounds like a longshot to me. Besides, you will not find posse members hiding out with gangs down in here. You know, they ought to have hung him in the first place. Saved everyone a heap of trouble."

"I reckon I'd have to agree with you there. Now, look who all he's killed, including kids. I'm tempted to find him and do the hanging myself, if it weren't sort of against the law I represent. As for finding posse members, once Herman White comes back to hisself, he can maybe tell us the names of the posse members. I'm going to see him next. But I want to talk to Jake Harper. He might be of some help to us, and we can put a stop to this."

NINE

ROSE GRUNTED AND STRUGGLED AGAINST the tight bindings.
Nothing gave. They'd really tied her tight this time. It hurt to breathe or
wiggle. Obviously, she wouldn't be able to get free on her own. Worse,
they were busy showing her what happened to one of the gang who did
something stupid.

They were hide-whipping the boy she'd tricked until she almost escaped. Situated so she had a good view of what they called Timmy's come-
uppance, she closed her eyes, but that didn't stop her hearing him yelp
every time the leather lash came down on his back. Even though he was
part of their gang, she was sorry she'd caused him to be punished like this.
Instead of being in a gang of thugs, he ought to be living at home and going
to school. Or working or doing something productive.

Soon as they finished, they'd be on her, so maybe she ought to be at
home pleasing some man. The only man who'd ever forced himself on her
was dead by her hand. She might not be able to make that happen here.
There were too many of them. Don't think about it. Don't.

It was the middle of the night before they finished with the poor boy,
and by then they were all so drunk they couldn't even stand upright. Even

the poor kid. Just as well for him, though. Finally, men were sprawled out on the wet ground like discarded garbage. On top of that, the stench of their campsite almost made her sick.

Wet, hogtied and nauseated as she was, she finally fell asleep. Tomorrow would have to take care of itself. In the middle of the night, she awoke, the pain of needing to relieve herself strong. A three-quarter moon hung high in the sky, casting shapes of the men, still unmoving humps on the ground. She had no choice, could hold it no longer. Good thing the night was warm, but just the same, it was humiliating to have to wet herself. It didn't make much difference. Her clothing was soaked from lying in an inch or more of rainwater.

All her life she'd faced anything and everything good or bad with a strong attitude, but it was all she could do not to break down and cry at the impossibility of her situation. To prevent that she studied her position in the light from the moon bright as day. There must be something. A way she could get out of this. A man sat beside poor battered Timmy patting the boys bleeding back with what looked like a rag. She'd seen him before and not too long ago. Then she remembered. He had been with Jake's gang along with a new man whose name she couldn't remember.

Was that the muffled slow clippity-clop of horses' hooves coming down the trail? Hope for help gave her new strength and she lifted her head. Two silhouettes, horses led by men, were on their way to where everyone was drunk out of their minds. How loud could she shout and not wake them? She had to get the attention of those two. Outlaws probably, but maybe she could gain their favor. Not every outlaw tied up women and took advantage of their helplessness. But if they knew who she was, they weren't likely to lift a finger. Bounty hunter? Enemy.

She dared not breathe while they snuck to the bottom, obviously on some sneaky mission, not wanting to be heard or to wake anyone. How great if they were coming in to start something and she could manage to escape.

Give them a few minutes to decide what they were going to do. They stood in one spot studying the layout around them. Though a small flame still flickered from the campfire, the gang sprawled well-hidden back of boulders big as houses. It was through a high gap she had spotted the intruders. They in turn crept closer to get a good look.

Though she took the chance that the newcomers might shoot her on sight, she tried to hail them.

"Hey, mister." Hell, she couldn't even hear herself. It'd have to be louder. Maybe a whistle or bird call would work. She remembered they'd used bird calls to get in with Jake's gang. Wonder where they were tonight?

Okay, here goes. A mourning dove was so common still she tried it several times. Then went right to the bob white. She hoped they would know those two birds didn't call out at night and know something was up. How did you warn bad men about bad men? Then escape both of them.

Once more she went through a long cycle of the two birds. Her only hope. One of the men turned to look in her direction through a gap and right at her. With the moon so bright, couldn't he see her trussed up to a tree like a gigantic cocoon? With the next calls she wiggled around as much as she could. Her face ought to reflect the moonlight. He had to see that someone was tied to a tree over here. What was wrong with him? Was he *blind?*

He kept looking her way, then punched his companion and pointed. They whispered a while, then started toward her. Yes, come on, keep coming. Yes, yes. Be quiet. Closer and closer. One dropped to his knees next to her and she let out a sigh of relief.

"Please get me out of here. Hurry. They're going to kill me. They're all drunk, but they could wake up any time now."

The man dragged out a huge knife and sawed away at the ropes while the other one kept watch.

At last, he took a quick look at her working her way out of the chopped-up rope and struggling to sit up. "Rose, is that you? My God, girl, how'd you get here like this?"

"Hsst, they'll hear you and they're a mighty mean gang of ugly men. Be quiet and get me out of here."

"Where's your horse?" This from the one on his knees finishing up his cutting job.

"Back at Cactus Junction. That's where they grabbed me."

"You're that lady bounty hunter, aren't you?"

"Keep talking so loud we'll all be trussed up like this, or you'll be dead. They're keeping me for some kind of special treat. Come on, let's get out of here."

"Rose, did you spot Jake or J. T. down here? These ole boys wouldn't go up against them."

"I was too busy defending myself and staying alive to notice anyone. Will you at least get us away from these men? Please."

A muffled shout came from the camp. Someone was awake and had spotted them. Her heart slammed around in her chest 'til it nearly choked her.

"Go on, Rose, hide, we'll handle this."

Three or four of the sleeping men crawled to their feet and stumbled around mostly talking nonsense. Still drunk as skunks. The big man who'd rode in with Dell went about gathering up guns all around the fire. Before the drunks noticed, he dumped them behind a crop of bushes and went back for more. Must've had them unarmed in a minute.

He finally returned with a saddled horse and handed her the reins. "We have got business here, but you mount up and ride out of here."

"I can't go off and leave you. Two against all them." She touched her hip but found no weapon.

"We'll take care of this. Git on out of here. Sheriff and I can handle it. Besides, they are already disarmed. Looks like you need you a gun. Hold on."

He disappeared into the melee, returning with a six-shooter. "Here girl, now scoot. I have to get in there and help him tie up this bunch. It's all took care of. Sheriff Dell says you scoot yourself outta here or you'll have him to deal with."

Relieved, she took the gun. Going unarmed would do her no good. Staying here would not help them.

" Always thought I could take care of myself, but sometimes—" She climbed into the saddle while babbling her tale.

The big man who had spotted her laid a hand on the horse's neck. "You did. If you had not used the bird calls, I would never have looked over here. It was very smart. I knew they did not call at night."

Reluctant to ride off she took up the reins. "What's your name?"

"I am Julio Jenkins."

For a moment she stared down at him, then she started to chuckle under her breath.

"What is so funny?"

"Ask your deputy when you get back."

She touched the horse's flank, and with one final check, she carefully guided it up the trail that led out of Palo Duro. A fresh wind scented with flowers of the plains cleansed her face of earlier tears. If she had anything to do with it, she would never return to this place. However, she had very little to do with what happened in her life. This experience had taught her that much, if nothing else.

She still had to pursue the man setting the fires, and though lawmen were after him as well, she might just get lucky and capture him before they did and earn the reward. Somehow, she had to locate those remaining posse members. It was very possible they had figured out they were targets and were protecting their homes and families. Still, as long as the arsonist remained free, she intended to try and catch him.

Breaking a few laws while hurting no one but yourself was one thing. Killing innocent and helpless children was quite another, and she couldn't abide it. Especially now that this man had included Mama in the victims. She would not take him alive.

DELL COULDN'T HELP CHUCKLING TO himself, seeing the confusion of the staggering outlaws searching for something to use to defend themselves against the two interlopers.

"That was sure a neat trick, Julio. Let's search this camp and have a setdown with these fellas. I'm anxious to see what they might know about our arsonist. He could be right here among them.

"I've been gone from home a long time and would like to get back to Guinn before she forgets what I look like, or various other things about me."

Julio laughed. "I would not mind going home, either, my friend. Little Dove feels the same about me, I am sure. So, let us get busy before the fire water drains away from their system, and they go silent on us."

"I suggest we play dumb at first, ask each one if they'd do such a thing. They might give up the real fire starter."

"That is a fine suggestion. Grab the most sober ones first before they get to where they can actually think. That one over there already standing might be a good place to begin."

"You take him, I'll get that one who's gone over to that tree to drain his pickle. Remember, we need to look for the arsonist or someone who knows the names of the posse who burnt him out."

Julio nodded and hurried to snatch the first man by the collar. Dell took off toward the one buttoning up his pants. A man who knew to do that was sober enough to talk straight.

He clamped fingers around the man's arm and jerked him so hard his feet left the ground. "What the—?" He swung his free fist toward Dell.

"Take 'er easy. Just want to ask you a few questions."

"I don't answer no questions from no—" He paused and peered at Dell. "Who are you, anyways? Come barging into our place."

"Let's just sit here on this log and relax. Me and my friend—that big man over there—we're hunting someone who's done something terrible. Something I'd hope you'd never do."

The man gaped at Dell who was glad of the moonlight since features told a lot about a man telling the truth or lying.

"What's that? I ain't done nothin'.""

"He's burning up women and little children."

"Naw, oh naw. You're right, I'd never... why, I've got me seven brothers and sisters, one still crawlin' around."

"Of course, I knew it, and I'll bet if you knew anyone doing that, you'd come right straight to me or my friend over there and tell us, wouldn't you?"

The man stared at the ground, and Dell gave him time to think. These men didn't want to squeal on their fellow outlaws.

He began to shake his head no.

Dell went right on. "Or maybe you'd just want to warn the folks that someone like this evil man was coming. Maybe you could help us do that?"

"Well, sure, but I can't squeal on no one."

"I understand. There was a bunch of men went in a posse to capture a killer, but instead of doing that something got out of hand and the man's house got set on fire. It burned up his wife and baby, and now he's doing the same all over the panhandle. If we could get the names of those who rode in the posse to warn them...." He looked square in the man's face and remained silent.

"Not to arrest them or anything? Just warn them he's coming?"

The man caught on quicker than Dell figured he would, coming out of a drunk.

"That's exactly right. You would warn these men, if you knew them, wouldn't you? Or tell us and we could warn them. The panhandle is a huge place, and sometimes posse members come from all over."

Again, the outlaw thought a while, then nodded. "Sure, if I ever seen 'em or anything, I'd warn them."

"Or if you found out or knew who they were you'd tell me or Marshal Jenkins over there?"

The man nodded vigorously, obviously relieved he wasn't being arrested.

Dell thanked him and patted him on the back. "The marshal there is at Hawkins Post, and I'm over in Saddler county at Thomas City. You tell your friends. If you tell us anything that stops this child burner there'd be a reward."

And so their work went with each gang member into the early morning, 'til the grumbling grew louder, and the men began to resist.

That's when Julio stood on a boulder, as if he weren't big enough already, and made an announcement. "Now, you boys can consider yourselves lucky we did not arrest you all and drag you in because we know you are outlaws. But we trust you to help us out with this, because you are not the kind of men who would set fire to women and children. Is that not right?"

By then it was apparent the outlaws were mostly sober and so relieved to learn they had escaped jail they'd agree to anything. This obvious by the shouting and cheering in reply to Julio's statement.

"Now, don't forget to tell all your friends about this, and remember there is a reward for stopping this man."

Dell rode out of Palo Duro beside Marshal Julio Perkins, not sure if what they had done would help them find either the arsonist or the families he intended to burn out, but a feller had to do something.

"It's too bad the rancher we helped out back there didn't know any of the other posse members. I'm wondering if he's just afraid to talk. He's taking his family to Lubbock to stay with their kin while he rebuilds. It occurs to me that he might know more than he would tell us, being in shock about his family almost dying in the fire and everything. Maybe we ought to visit him again. After his family is no longer in danger, who knows? He might give us some posse names so we could figure out how to catch this devil."

Dell rode alongside the silent Indian. Seemed like he was doing most of the talking.

"You know, Julio, the hardest thing about finding these boys who rode out that day is they know they done wrong burning that man's place, and they don't want to face the consequences. Chances are they've gone into hiding from the law. Maybe not even in their own home. Maybe they're hunkered down a week's ride from here and don't know what's happening about these fires. What if we put out a poster giving them immunity if they turn themselves in so we can stop the burning? Just say on it that their homes are burning, and they need to come in so we can help stop that. I can't figure out how our fire starter knows who they are."

"Me, either. That has puzzled me. But you know, all he needs is to have recognized one or two. He could then scare them into giving him other names before he kills them."

Well, at least he was finally talking. "True, each of the posse members would know some of the others. If he promised not to kill their family, they'd tell him, then he'd go ahead and kill them anyway. It's been a puzzlement for all of us, but this has got to be what's happening. I'm pleased we were able to talk about this." Dell reined his horse around a good-sized rock on the trail. "I think I'll go home to my wife for a few days. We can put up posters in Saddler County right way and hope we get some results. We're just chasing our tails out here now.

"But I'm gonna swing by that burned out ranch first, talk to Herman White. He was sending his family to relatives but sounded like he planned to stay. He might just be gonna hunt down this mad dog killer himself. Maybe I can get something out of him."

Julio nodded. "I have to return to my duties, but I wish you luck. Should a fire happen again, let me know. I will help out. Otherwise let us visit in a week or two. Once I can get away, I would be happy to come to your place to see how things are going with our new plans."

Dell squinted up at a flock of crows swirling from one tree to another, their loud caws echoing in the warm spring morning. "You'd be welcome there, marshal."

Though he yearned to go home and hold Guinn in his arms and sleep in a bed with her tucked against him, he had to follow his hunch and talk to Herman White. The ground was getting a little too hard and too lonely, but he was responsible for the people in his county.

The smell of smoke still hung in the air when Dell rode up to the White ranch. How sad it looked, burnt timbers piled where the barn and house once stood. An iron bedstead stood mournfully in what was once the couple's bedroom, a cast iron stove and scattered utensils marked the kitchen. The place was deadly still, but far out in the pasture some cattle grazed, a horse among them.

He shouted hello so as not to get shot at. Hailed Herman once. Finally, the man, looking years older than when he'd first met him just a few days earlier, came out of the trees alongside the yard carrying a rifle at his side. Must be sleeping out. Lying in wait perhaps?

Dell raised a hand. "It's me, Sheriff Hoffman, Mister White. Come to see how you're making out.

They shook hands.

"Didn't know you at first. The man who saved my wife and babe. I'll always be grateful. Sorry I didn't say so then, it was such a frightful time."

"I understand, sir. I wanted to ask you something, if you don't mind."

"I reckon I owe you a lot more than the answer to a question. Ask away."

"I wonder, did you maybe know any of the other posse members from that night?"

Herman's face went blank. "I was mending a fence, Sheriff."

White had misunderstood him. "Well, sir, I mean the night Amos Horner's ranch was burned out."

"I had nothing in this world to do with that, sir. I swear I didn't. When I heard about it, I was sick. True, I ride with plenty of posses. I like to help out the law where I can, but I didn't go that night."

"I'm sorry, sir. You didn't ride with the posse that pursued and burnt down Amos Horner's ranch?"

Herman blanched, raised the rifle in a threatening position, the barrel all but pointing straight at him.

Dell raised both palms in defense. "Hold it, there, mister. You don't want to do that. You have a family who needs you. If you weren't with them, can you tell me about what happened that night?"

"I sure as hell can, but you might not believe me. The wife was birthing that night, so when they came calling, knowing I was one who would normally go along, I turned them down to stay with her. You can ask...." He paused and looked all around. Then, with tears in his eyes, went on. "No, you can't ask them. They're gone from here. I don't know if we'll ever get this place back together. But that's my story and I swear it's the truth."

Of course, he believed him. No one could lie so convincingly. However, he still might be able to identify one or more of the riders from that fateful night. "I do believe you, Mister White, but could you tell me some of the names of the men who did ride that night? We already know five, no you're number six, but there are still quite a few left."

"If I do, you're gonna go and arrest them for killing that woman and child, aren't you? I know that wasn't right, it's horrible. But I can't. I can't. Don't you see? I have enough troubles without getting that bunch after me. too?"

Dell sighed. The man hadn't denied it that time. But no sense in arguing round and round the point. Damn, this was a big problem. But he had to try one more time. "Tell you what. Just give me one name and we'll get him to help us trap this man when he comes to burn his ranch. That way you'll be saving the man's ranch, and we won't arrest him if he helps. How is that?"

Hope flared in Herman White's sad eyes. "I don't know if I can trust you. I want to help you. If I do, will it save the other ranchers, or will you arrest every one of them for doing their duty? The fire was an accident, it had to be. I can't see any one of those men doing it on purpose. What this fire starter is doing is no accident. He is deliberately murdering innocent people."

As an enforcer of the law, Dell couldn't make such a promise without lying. He was right about the guilt of Amos Horner. But still, those men had burned to death a woman and her baby. Whether on purpose or as an accident, they had to pay. Perhaps not with their lives—if they could prove they didn't know the family was inside, but with some prison time.

If he lied to Herman White, then what did that make him?

Sometimes he walked a very fine line between the law, what was right and what was wrong.

His hesitation told the man more than words could.

"I'm sorry, I can't give you any names, but I can steer you in the right direction. The next ranch over is empty now for good reason, and that's all I can say. Now, if you would please ride on. And you go with my most grateful thanks for what you did. I just wish I could help you more."

Bidding him goodbye and good luck, Dell rode off toward the ranch White had indicated. It wouldn't do much good if it were empty. Amos probably wouldn't bother burning one with no one in it. He appeared to be more set on killing by waiting 'til evening or night when the family was all inside. No, Amos was a killer, through and through.

Still, he went by the ranch—the S Bar H the ragged signpost said—and looked around. White was correct. They must've heard the news of the burnings. They'd cleared out lock, stock, and barrel. Not even a curtain left on a window. It wasn't much of a place, but still a home. The ram-shackle barn was empty of anything. This was more a start-up farm than a well-tended ranch. Amos wouldn't bother when he caught sight of it, if he hadn't already.

Tired to the bone, Dell started home. He could only hope that the word had reached all the others who rode that fateful night, and they were all taking precautions. Without knowing more, there wasn't much he could do. It was almost dark the next evening when he rode up to his house. Guinn must've heard him coming, for she ran off the porch to greet him. The wind caught her red hair and blew strands around her face. She smiled up at him. "I'm so happy to see you home. I worried something might have happened. But you're here now."

"We've had some experiences." He couldn't wait to dismount and take her in his arms. Together they walked to the barn, took care of Curly's needs, then went to the house. That night it was good to crawl into his own bed next to his sweet wife. She was real happy to see him, too.

TEN

BARS OF SUNLIGHT AND THE old red rooster crowing awoke Dell. The feather bed felt much better to his weary muscles than the rocky ground. So did the warmth of Guinn's body curled against his backside.

"You awake?" Her lips nibbling his ear sent an urgent need through him, and he turned to take her in his arms.

Later, while eating breakfast, he discussed his worries about the arsonist with Guinn. She often came up with good suggestions for solving his problems.

"I just need to find one man who knows the names of the posse so we can set a trap at one of the ranches he hasn't burned yet. If we don't, he will kill more families."

She spread grape jam over her biscuit. "Don't you think the men who rode in the posse know what's going on by now?"

"If they stayed in touch with each other, maybe. But getting one of them to talk is impossible." Dell sprinkled pepper over his biscuits and gravy and took a big bite, washing it down with coffee before going on. He told her about Herman White.

"The panhandle is big country. Their ranches are liable to be scattered miles apart and they never come in contact with each other. They could just be carrying out their business and unaware of this man's need for revenge 'til he sneaks up one night and sets fire to one of their homes. Or, like I said, if they do know, they aren't about to tell me."

"Someone besides one who actually rode with them must know at least one or two of them."

He put down his fork and glanced at her. "I know, that's what's so frustrating. Who might that be?

"Who got up the posse in the first place? Do they keep records of the men who show up?"

"Not always. Everything is hectic. The word goes out, and whoever's in the area and hears about it might join up to run down the killer. Or, as the posse passes through, they saddle up and join it. No one has come forward to admit organizing the posse. Everyone involved feels guilty about what happened. It could be any number of men from lots of places. John Smith could've been in town from thirty miles away and volunteered to take part." He scooted back his chair. "Well, we've put up posters for anyone knowing anything about who rode out that day, but I'm not holding my breath. What they did was horrible, and none of them will ever want to admit they were a part of it. I'm hoping someone who did not join up will know something."

He kissed her on the cheek and fetched his hat from the rack next to the front door. "I'll be home this evening. If anything comes up, I'll let you know. Have a good day."

"I will. Some of us ladies are getting together to quilt after we finish our morning chores. I'll be at Beth Staymore's if you need me. But I'll have your supper on the table at the usual time."

He smiled, kissed the tips of his finger and threw her a kiss before going out into the sunny day. Somehow, he needed to learn who was setting the fires and put a stop to it. Just because he'd come home to Thomas City didn't mean he'd given up finding this mean old scudder.

He thought about what Guinn had said, that someone who hadn't ridden with them knew who at least one of the members was. He just had to figure out how to get in touch with who that might be and convince them to give out some names. Better yet, find out where the known killer was hiding out. Though, by now, most had figured out who must be setting the fires, since he had been convicted of killing that man over in Amarillo. Yet no one could seem to figure out where he might be. And as far as anyone knew, he had his son with him.

Two strangers wandering around amongst people who all knew each other. How were they keeping hidden?

Dell walked his rounds of town as usual before going to his office to see what might have come up overnight. If anything of great importance happened, he'd have been awakened, so things must've been quiet.

His deputy, Brand Kingsley, and the jailer, Guy Goodson, reported all was fairly quiet.

He hung up his hat, sat behind his desk and rifled through a few papers that had piled up while he was gone. "What do you mean, fairly quiet?"

They both began to talk at once, and he put up a hand. "In the jail or on the street?"

"Jail."

"Street." They spoke together.

"Guy first." He stared at his jailer.

Before the man could open his mouth, Dutch, his other deputy, burst into the office. "Say, did you hear what happened down at the mercantile last night?"

Guy lifted both hands. "I was fixin' to tell him when you butted in."

"Wait, hold it. First, it's the jail, now it's the mercantile. Is this what you call fairly quiet? And why wasn't I called out?"

Dutch planted his skinny butt on the corner of the desk. "This kid broke in. Someone saw him. One of the doves of the night. Anyway, she came running and told me. I went down and caught the poor hungry bugger hid-

ing in a corner, his arms full of cans and shaking like a leaf in a windstorm."
He stopped, took a breath.

Dell studied each man in turn. "Continue please." By now, he was ready
to holler at someone, but he held his temper and waited.

Everyone looked at Guy who shrugged. "My turn? Okay, Dutch
brings this boy in and he's sitting back there in a cell, calm as you please.
All he wanted was something to eat. He looks and acts half starved. Not
real clean either. So, I sent out for some breakfast for him. Didn't see
no reason at all for calling you when he come peaceful. No gunplay nor
nothin'. You been riding all day yesterday, so we figgered, me and Dutch
figgered it'd wait 'til today." He took a deep breath and sank down in a
chair in the corner.

Dell wiped his forehead with the palm of one hand. Dang, it was good
to be back to normal situations. "Well, I'll talk to the boy, see what can be
done about his situation. Anyone get his name?" His glance brought no
reply. "Okay, I'll find out. Reverend Makers will see the hungry family re-
ceives some food and maybe other help. No one's going hungry in Saddler
County if I can help it. Let's see if we can find out who this boy is, give him
a talk about stealing, and get him home to his parents.

 Guy hurried in front of Dell into the back of the office where the cells
were. "He's real scared. Ain't talking to no one."

Dell shooed the jailer back. "Just scared, that's all. I'll handle this." It
wasn't that he'd had much experience with kids. He and Guinn didn't have
any children. His eyes teared. Well, not anymore, but he could deal with
one scared kid, surely.

The wide-eyed boy was scooted as far back in the corner of the tiny cell
as could be. He was older than Dell had expected from their descriptions.
Maybe sixteen, seventeen, gaunt, dirty and terrified out of his mind. It happened no one was locked up, right now, but him.

"Howdy, boy." Dell took the large key off the wall across from the cell.

"You git out of here and leave me alone." The kid kicked out as if to defend himself, his voice thick and angry. "We ain't done nothin' and neither has anyone I know, so I can't squeal. And I sure ain't talking to no sheriff."

"Now, son, no need to get upset. I want to help you."

"Don't son me. I said leave me alone. My daddy will come break me out of here, and he'll shoot the lot of you wearin' them badges."

Well, this wasn't going to be as easy as he'd hoped. "If you'll tell me your name and your daddy's name, I'll notify him you're here and he can come get you out. I'm sure he doesn't want to shoot a sheriff, or anyone else for that matter."

"I ain't telling nobody my daddy's name. Go away or maybe he'll cut your throat for botherin' me. Shoot you dead or maybe burn your houses —uh—like that other fella."

Shocked at the threat that hit so close to home, Dell backed off. This could take some looking into before he let this boy loose or contacted his daddy, if the kid ever gave up his name. Maybe, when the kid settled down a bit from the fright of being caught in the act of stealing, he could get somewhere with him.

Wonder where he got that idea? Burn our houses? Could'a just heard talk around town, but it was pretty suspicious. He'd give him a chance to cool down then talk to him some more. The little rascal just could know something about the arsonist. Did he dare think he could be the arsonist's son? Surely not.

He shrugged, hung the key back where it was, and returned to his office to go over the new wanted posters delivered by the stage while he was gone.

One of them contained a crude rendering of Amos Horner, the killer escaped from prison who was now the only suspect in building fires that were killing people. As such, the reward had been increased from the original two thousand dollars to five thousand, but the picture wasn't any better. He was ugly, had two eyes, a nose and mouth, and scraggly hair. And, oh yeah, two ears. That was all that could be said from the drawing.

Dell wanted to catch this man in the worst way but doing so was proving way more difficult than he'd thought it would. Maybe this reward increase would bring some snake out of the grass. That much money could be mighty tempting.

ROSE LEFT THE BORROWED HORSE at the livery in Cactus Junction and paid for another night for Cimarron who'd been deserted when she was snatched. She was about as dirty as a body could get. It was like she needed new skin. The way those men had tossed her all over the place and pawed around on her, she wanted shut of the clothes she wore too, so on the way to the bath house, she made one stop.

A bell tinkled above the door of the gentleman's clothing store above her head. There was always a particular odor to clothing stores. Probably appeared stronger because she wasn't in one very often. She went directly to the britches folded and stacked by size on a table. A clerk sidled his way to stand beside her. Then changed his mind and stepped back. Smelled her, no doubt.

"Are you buying for your husband or perhaps father?" His voice came out his nose or appeared to.

"No. You see what I'm wearing?"

He had pretended not to notice, or at least not to judge her choice in pants. Looking her up and down, he replied without hesitation, "I presumed, ma'am, that you were caught out without proper garb and borrowed those. And that you wanted to go in the door down the street a ways where you could replace your clothing with proper attire."

She drew herself up so that her full six feet towered over the little twerp. "Is that the way you keep good customers, with sarcasm?"

He flushed bright red. "I beg your pardon. I really thought someone was pulling a joke on me and sent you in here to see what I would do. You really wish to replace what you're wearing with similar attire?" He chortled. "I'm so sorry. Let me show you some trousers I believe you'll like. They have just come in and are the latest style."

He lifted one pair and fingered the fabric. "With summer coming on these will be perfect. They are woven linen, and this blue would pick up the color of your eyes." He actually winked at her.

If he wasn't very careful, she would slap him silly, or better yet sock him one in the jaw. But the britches did feel so good and cool to the touch. "I'll try on a pair."

Together they picked through for trousers long enough for her. Then she chose a shirt of a brighter blue and one of crimson, went behind the curtain and put them on, donning the blue shirt to compliment her eyes just to make him more uncomfortable. She added stockings but ignored his offer of garters to hold them up. "I will however need undergarments." She eyed him for a smart remark, but he simply found her what she asked for. By then she was hoping for an excuse to pop him one, his flirting was so evident.

However, two men entered to buy trousers, and he made short work of taking her money and wrapping her purchases. They must've been good customers because he left her immediately to fawn over them both.

The bell tinkled her departure, and she burst out laughing. No man had flirted with her since she began wearing britches and carrying a gun, which of course was absent here in town, and it was funny for some reason. Perhaps her emotions were simply releasing all their pent-up relief at still being alive after her recent experience with those outlaws. Mostly, she was still puzzled as to why they had chosen to grab her. There must have been a reason, but she wanted only to run down Amos Horner and carry his hairy head to the marshal's office. Nothing else mattered any longer.

Carrying her packages, she hurried across the street and inside the bath house where the steam from other bathers held the fragrance of sweet-scented lye soap.

The attendant poured hot water in a large tub, and she stripped off her filthy clothing, crawled in and stretched out full length in the tin tub. How heavenly. She scrubbed clean then remained there 'til goose bumps popped out. Then she climbed out and slipped into the lovely clean new clothes.

How was she going to go about finding this Amos Horner? It was like he'd disappeared from the entire state. Wonder if he still had the kid they'd claimed survived the fire the posse set, or if he'd abandoned him somewhere. Wish she knew how old he was.

Worse yet, she couldn't even find anyone who'd admit to knowing the man. Because he escaped before they got him locked up in prison there was no one to ask there who might have got to know him. This was a tough one, but she'd solve it, one way or another.

On occasion, outlaws liked to be around other outlaws if only to brag about their latest job, how much money or how scared their victims were. Stuff like that. And those men were not likely to squeal on each other. But everyone liked to brag about knowing someone like Amos, even when it wasn't wise. There was one gang she might get something out of if she got lucky. The outlaw, Jake Harper, trusted her not to haul one of them in, no matter the reward. That was because they'd grown up together.

Sitting at a dinner table in one of the many saloons that happened to serve the best food in Cactus Junction, she made her decision. She'd find Jake, and that wouldn't be too hard 'cause she knew his habits. After he pulled a job, his favorite hideout was Palo Duro Canyon. Only the law couldn't seem to learn that.

However, there was one problem. That bunch that hauled her off down there just a few days ago might still be there. It was a bit scary thinking of returning there. The canyon was huge. Charlie Goodnight owned a tremendous ranch in there, and you had to stay away from trespassing, or getting caught at it. Outlaws hung out mostly throughout one section where the Comanche had lived until they were driven out. Bluffs and rock formations provided good hiding places.

Getting into the cutback Jake liked to call his cave without anyone spotting her could be difficult. She'd been in there earlier without any problems, so it was worth a try. Maybe she ought to go in disguise. A woman in a dress wasn't a good idea, so why not as a man? She liked to wear britches, was comfortable in them. Only trouble might be her hair and these danged breasts. They always revealed her to be a woman. Pin her hair up or cut it to shoulder length where a lot of men wore theirs. She'd heard talk of women going to battle during the war. They bound their breasts flat to avoid being detected.

She could do the same. Then go down there and hang around, perhaps find someone who knew of Amos and where he might be. Though weak, it was a place to start.

By the next evening, she'd picked up Jake Harper's trail. He and some of his gang went into Carlton the day before, robbed a rich rancher who'd come in on the stage and walked home carrying a case of money after he sold a prize bull. It was being told all around town that several down and out families had received a few hundred dollars each deposited on their back porch. Of course, Jake took credit for it by leaving his calling card—the Jack of spades.

Knowing Jake as she did, she dropped in at the Golden Mule where one of his best pals worked. Two-Dice Cash was working the craps table where he could be found most every night. She stood at the table for a while until she caught his eye.

"Hidee, Rosie gal. Haven't seen you in a while."

"You just haven't been looking. I was down at the canyon just last week visiting with Jake."

"Oh, sure you was." He slid several chips over the ten and watched while the dice rolled, coming up eight. "Sheeit."

"Two-Dice, I need to see Jake again. I heard about yesterday. Did he go back to the canyon?"

The little man looked all around. "Be still, gal. You know where Jake is.

Where he goes after, you know. All I'm sayin'. He tapped a red square on the table. "Now get on away so I can win me some money."

She patted his shoulder. "Thanks. See you around."

Not at Palo Duro. Jake'd be hiding out in his favorite place on the Red River. Two-Dice told her as much as he would. The next morning, she headed out to pay a casual visit to her old friend. She easily spotted the gang's usual hideout above the Red River where guards were posted and maneuvered past them to find a celebration going on.

Jake slapped his thigh and laughed. "Come to put my head in a tow sack, Rosie, or join the party?"

"Reckon I ought to do the first, but I'll let it go this time, seein' as how you've been so generous with folks. I heard you from the rise over yonder. Aren't you afraid someone will come along and tell the law?"

"Naw, not tonight, nothing could go wrong tonight."

"How's that? You got a guardian angel or something?"

"No, I got good friends. Gonna protect me from harm. One's the sheriff."

"Jake, don't tell me you bought off the sheriff of Carlton?"

He nodded and laughed. "All it takes is lots of money and the promise of more."

"Well, I hate to tell you, but he was killed last week in a gunfight or something. Anyway, someone shot him dead. But I wouldn't be too worried, I met one of his deputies who seems to be dumb as a bag of rocks."

"Aw, shit. You don't say." He threw back his head and laughed. "Dangerous job, being a lawman. Well, we'll just have to make hay while the sun shines, so to speak. Maybe the new one will like us just as well." He was just drunk enough to tell her the truth. Maybe he'd tell her what he might know about Amos and where he could be. It was possible.

"Well get on down off that magnificent animal and join us." She climbed off Cimarron and joined the drinkers.

Sharing a bottle of rotgut whiskey with Jake she took in the faces right quick. Good thing it wasn't dark yet, she could get a good look at each and every one. All looked familiar. Being quiet she leaned close to him. "I thought I saw a new feller with you last time, over there in Palo Duro. What become of him?"

"Don't know who you could mean, Rosie, you know I'm plumb tight about welcoming strangers."

"Seems like I remember his name was Iverson, something like that. Where'd he come from?"

Jake took a long pull from the bottle. "Hell, Rosie, I don't know, can't remember. That was back a ways, and I've had too much of this." He held up the whiskey, then took another swig. "'Sides, I want to talk about something else."

"What might that be?"

"Want to ask if they've put out any new 107anted on me or any of my gang." He laughed loud. "Was hoping my hide would get to where it was worth more if I kept on stealing and giving it to the poor. Thought I might catch up with ole Jesse and Frank. I'd sure like to be as famous as they are 'fore I die."

"Dang it, Jake. You get that famous someone will sure turn you in for the reward and you'll get your wish. You haven't seen any strangers riding the trail or pulling little jobs here lately, have you?"

"You know I always keep my head down. Wouldn't turn in a fellow outlaw, anyway."

She studied his familiar face. Spoke softly. "Not even if he was killing kids. Little kids and innocent women?"

"Shit, Rosie. I didn't know they was such a thing as innocent women." He poked his elbow in the ribs of the man next to him and guffawed. "Hear that? Innocent women. Come on, Rosie. Have another drink, and don't be so serious."

Her heart sank. Jake had changed since the war. Was a time he wouldn't have acted like this. 'Course, he'd lost his entire family during that blasted war, so it was hard to blame him for being ornery. Still, she wished he was still so happy-go-lucky as he'd been before he marched off to kill himself some Yankees. Darned shame. She slipped away from him. A man nearby backed off as well. Who was he? She'd seen him the last time she was with the gang but couldn't quite place him. She would, though. Soon as she thought about him. She hardly ever forgot anyone she'd met.

Meanwhile, she ought to punch Jake for being such a harebrain, and because she'd learned absolutely nothing.

Without bidding any of the drunken bunch goodbye, she fetched Cimarron and rode off. The moon came up, sending golden ripples along the length of the Red River. The night was silent, the only sound that of the horse's hooves rattling in the gravel of the shoreline. Made her feel lonely. Sometimes it wasn't as exciting as she'd hoped, chasing all over the countryside after outlaws and making money doing it. Yet on a beautiful night like this, how could she regret the decision?

She reined the gelding south toward Thomas City. Time she checked in with Dell to see if there'd been any sign of Amos down that way. Maybe the two of them together could catch up with him before he did more harm.

ELEVEN

SOMEONE SHOUTED HIS NAME AND banged on the door. Dell grumbled, fumbled and came awake. Hopping on one foot then the other, he stuffed each leg into his britches, grabbed a shirt off the back of the bedroom chair and hobbled barefoot through the house yelling.

"Stop that infernal racket. I'm coming, I'm coming. On my way. What in thunder—?"

He threw open the door. Both his night deputy, Dutch, and Whit Burns, the town marshal, leaped around on his front porch.

"Sheriff, sheriff, the mercantile's on fire. We got bucket brigades but knew you'd want to know." Both men shouted the garbled words, so they barely made sense.

Guinn came rushing in behind him, shrugging into a robe and carrying his boots. "Here, here. What do you need? Breakfast, coffee?"

He took the boots, sat briefly to stomp them onto his feet. "No, no. Thanks. Go on back to bed. No sense in you being up, too." He kissed her on the cheek and hurried out the door, running beside the two men down the street toward the blaze that leaped high into the dark sky.

In the light from the fire, lines of men passed buckets of water from nearby watering troughs to pour on the blaze. It was like pissing on the roaring flames.

Dear God, there wasn't enough water in every trough in town to put that damn thing out.

Still, sweat pouring, he joined the line, everyone doing what they could 'til the fire won the battle and the supply of water and men were both exhausted. One by one they dropped to the wet ground, eyes reflecting the blaze that had defeated all their efforts. The town's only mercantile lay in smoking bones.

"What in the world happened?" The storekeeper swore in a loud voice, threw his empty bucket and sat beside them. "I swear there wasn't a spark of fire in any lamp when we closed down. No fire in the stove, either. I swear, Sheriff." Tears in his eyes he swept a hand over his bald head. "What could've started this?"

"Maybe someone dropped a match without blowing it out."

"I swear no one lit a match. I was the last one out." He jumped to his feet. "Did anyone see anything? Anything at all?"

One by one the men shook their heads, a murmur passing among them.

Suspicion built a growing doubt in Dell's mind, but first things first. He finally rose, taking charge from the store owner. "First thing tomorrow, every man who can get loose from his work show up to help clean up this mess." He wouldn't yet voice his deep-set feeling that this was no accident.

Ancell, who owned the sawmill south of town was the first to offer help. "My man will start cutting timber to rebuild. Anyone who can help, it'd be appreciated."

A murmur of agreement came from the weary men.

Dell thanked him. "We'll divide into a clean-up crew and a building crew. I've put in some time lumbering, so I'll help with the sawing. We can begin as soon as the coals burn out. Don't you worry none, we'll do all we can."

By sunup, men were busy all over the ruins of the store. At noon, it looked like every woman in town turned up with food and drinks for the working men. That evening, Dell and Guinn trudged home side by side. She'd been right with him all afternoon helping.

She wiped her face of grit. "How do you think that started?"

"It's hard to say. I have my suspicions, but I hate to blame anyone 'til I can look into it some more."

"You think someone started it deliberately. Why would anyone do that?"

"Why does anyone start fires?"

"I'll get you something to eat while you clean up. I can have a bath after you've gone to work. I know you have so much to get done."

"I don't know what I'd do without you, Guinn. I can just grab some left-over biscuits and butter, maybe some coffee. You go on and clean up. I know how you women are about being dirty."

In spite of the tragic circumstances, both chuckled about his remark. "Oh, you do know about us women, do you? I can wash my hands and face, make you some eggs and gravy to go with those biscuits. Go on and clean up while I do, old man."

"Old man? Is that what you think. I'll have you know I won't be forty for six years. Is that old?" While he cleaned up at the wash pan, he wondered aloud about the fire. "If it's who I think it was, we've got us a real problem." Yet he didn't want to voice his opinion 'til he did some checking.

"Well, I know you have to keep your suspicions to yourself, but I hope whatever you think isn't true, if it's going to bring everyone loads of trouble. Here, your breakfast is ready. Come eat and be on your way."

A short while later, Dell hurried down the street and stomped into the office. All his men were waiting. Brand, Dutch, Guy and the town marshal, Whit, all crowded into the small room.

Brand spoke up. "We can form a posse to get out there and see if we can find this fellow. Who would do something like this? There's plenty of mean varmints running around in gangs. We can round them all up."

Dell held up a hand. "Let's just think this over first. What about the kid you found broke into the mercantile night before last? How did he act? What did he look like? We turned him loose the next morning, did he say anything to any of you?"

Dutch was the first to come to the boy's defense. "Aw, dang. He was such a scrawny, scared child. I can't see him doing such a thing. He was just hungry, that's all."

Dell tapped his desktop. "I didn't ask for opinions. Answer my questions. How did he act? When did you let him out of jail? What did he say? Make any threats?"

"He was quiet all night, sleeping most of the time. I let him out yesterday morning when I went off shift, like you said, Sheriff. He just ran off. Never said anything untoward."

Whit, who had only been hired as town marshal a few months earlier, spoke up. "Well, I'm sure of one thing. Townsfolk wouldn't deliberately destroy the only place they can buy their goods. Doesn't make any sense."

Dell agreed. His money was on the boy.

Brand went to look out the window. "I hate to say this 'cause it could mean whole towns burning down, but you reckon the fire starter done it?"

"Nah, the fire starter's on a vengeance trail and no one in this town has done anything to him." He paused, studied his men a moment. "Reckon he could've got mad 'cause we put his boy in jail. That might be enough to set him off. Sure, as I'm the sheriff of this county, I'll find out who did this and make sure they pay. Him or someone else. Dadgum, someone had to see something." He took a deep breath to settle down then went on.

"It's our duty to figure out who did it and ride out to arrest them. There's plenty of folks working on restoring the mercantile. Everyone will want justice. We'll leave one lawman here to take care of things and the rest of us will start investigating."

Dell assigned each man a section of town. "Go door to door. Talk to everyone who might have seen something or heard someone make a threat. We'll run down this maniac."

Damn, he hoped he was right, and it wasn't the fire starter or his boy. On the other hand, having someone else in the county starting fires was scary as heck. Just have to keep checking it out 'til the guilty person was found. What a mess. A terrible mess.

His men spread out, each taking a section of town where the clues were most likely to be found. Folks who lived out of town would be questioned next, though they were least likely to have seen or heard anything that night. All the same, no one would be missed.

Late that evening, everyone returned with only one piece of information. The blacksmith saw the boy trudge past his place and out of town the morning he was released. A disappointed group of lawmen gathered once more in the sheriff's office.

"Okay, men, I know nothing to do but run down this Amos Horner. He needs caught, anyway, but I want one of you to remain here and be vigilant in case this ornery ruffian returns to cause more trouble for our town. It's time this Horner was put out of business.

"I see there's a good crew working on rebuilding the mercantile, so let's go about our business of catching this fire starter." He left Guy, his jailer, in charge so the deputies and marshal could take part in an all-out search for Amos Horner and his son.

Tired but resolved, he walked home to spend his last evening with Guinn for a spell. No telling how long it would take to catch Horner.

He sat at the supper table, bringing her up to date on things. "I know precisely where we'll start this hunt. We're going to find that Amos Horner, 'cause he's number one on my list, and his boy, too. I'm afraid he's responsible for the mercantile fire."

She shook her head sadly and sipped her iced tea. "Looks like I'll be taking care of things around this place by myself for a while." She kissed the back of his hand. "I can handle it just fine, so don't you worry one bit about me."

He grinned. One thing he never worried about was Guinn handling things. Still, he sure hated having to ride out once more and leave her to it. But like she always said, she married a lawman and had to expect him to do his job. In fact, she often bragged that it made her proud when he brought in a lawbreaker and made life safer in the small town. He'd married the right woman. That was for sure.

The next morning, Dell, Dutch, Brand and Whit saddled up, loaded a rented pack horse with their necessities and rode out in serious search of Amos Horner. They aimed to stop at Hawkins Post and ask Julio if his cousin, Angelo, could join them in the search. Angelo was one heck of a tracker and could pick up his trail if anyone could. It was past time to get serious about catching this arsonist.

They rode into Hawkins Post late, but the saloon was still open.

Dell gestured toward the lamplight and open door. "Don't know about you boys, but I've got a dusty taste in my mouth. We may be sleeping out under the stars tonight seeing as how it's so late, and there's few lodgings here."

"Well, I'll buy that." Brand slipped down to the ground, the first to head into the saloon.

The other two echoed the suggestion and moved to the hitching rail.

"Say, Dell, ain't that Rosie's hoss yonder? Did you know she was here?" Whit reined up and climbed down off his pony. "Whew, I'm glad to get off that fool horse. Got to get me a better mount. This un stomps around like a danged pinto pony."

Brand laughed. "Well, it is a pinto pony. You get him for your fifteenth birthday or what?"

Dell chuckled. At the same time, he studied the gleaming red coat and black points that marked Rosie's true bay horse. "Yep, that's her horse. Cimarron's an Andalusian bay, and a beauty not to be mistaken anywhere, even at rest standing hipshot at a hitching rail. You want a fine riding animal, get you one of them, but good luck finding one."

Following Dell, Whit, Brand and Dutch admired the tall bay's configuration. "Don't see many of them here in Texas." Dell stepped up on the boardwalk and peered over the swinging doors of the saloon.

"Don't see any of them in Texas, I'd wager. Where'd she get such an animal? Killing for bounty don't pay that good, does it?" Dutch admired the horse, its deep red coat gleaming in the sunlight.

Dell tied up his own fine mount, Curly. He'd been a gift from the town when his beloved Burt was shot and killed a couple of years earlier. "Naw, one of her friends, when she worked for her mama in Fort Smith, gave it to her. Come on, let's go in and join her, maybe she's heard some talk about Amos. I know she'd like to get her hands on him for the bounty. Wonder if she's heard the amount has been upped."

"Bounty hunters make more dough than we ever thought of." The grumble came from town marshal Whit Burns who clearly envied Rose her horse but did not respect the way she earned her living.

A good crowd inside made enough noise that Dell didn't bother to try to answer Whit's gripe. Everyone had something bad to say about someone. He, for one, liked Rose. Though she had a twisted belief in justice, at times, he agreed with her that the law wasn't always right. Something he couldn't admit out loud.

SINCE SHE ALWAYS SAT WITH her back to the wall, Rose spotted Dell the moment he and the lawmen from Saddler County sauntered through the doors. He acknowledged her with the raise of his hand, and she beckoned them all to join her.

They did, dragging one more chair to the table which put Whit with his back to the door, but Brand and Dutch were sideways, which meant they could cover the marshal should a Hickok situation come up. The comparison amused her, yet it was a common superstition for many ever since Wild Bill had been shot holding aces and eights, coincidentally with his back to the door of a saloon in Deadwood. Whit Burns obviously either didn't know about it or didn't care.

After ordering beers all around, Dell greeted her warmly, causing the others to stare. Clearly, they didn't understand the friendship between the two, or they didn't approve.

A girl in a fancy dress with a low-cut neckline brought beers with two-inch heads on, but the men, fresh off an all-day ride, didn't object.

"Rosie, we saw Cimarron outside, but I didn't expect to see you hanging around here after your—uh—adventure."

She whipped a hand through the air. "Oh, that? It was nothing, but I wouldn't pay to see it happen to anyone else."

For a while, they discussed the bunch who had grabbed her. "Must be new to the area not to know no better than to grab our Rosie." Dell turned to her, serious as could be. "Reckon you haven't heard any more about that fella who's starting fires."

"Well, now, I'm surprised you'd think I'd be hanging about here if I knew where to find that scudder." She finished her glass of ale in one long swallow. "Want to hunt him down together? Give you half the reward. That's a lot of money."

"Why would you do that, Rose?" Dell wiped off his beer-head moustache."Cause you have more connections than I do. Maybe we could find him faster."

"Got any ideas— any at all? Something has to be done. I'm thinkin' he could've burnt the mercantile in Thomas City, but even if not, he's guilty of the others." Frowning, he scratched up under his Stetson.

"When did he burn the mercantile?"

"The other night. We're after who did it but can't prove he did."

"Well, Dell, who else is going around burning stuff?"

"Yeah, but ranches and for revenge. Can't see a connection."

She nodded and sipped at her beer. Wiping her lips, she studied him closely. "You really think you've got another firebug in Saddler County?"

"I'm hoping not. We have to run this man down 'fore he burns up half the county. I want to see him hung for all the killings he's done."

Rosie shook her head. "Well, to tell the truth, I might have someone we could go to. Not sure, but he used to ride in every posse he could, and I learned this morning that he hasn't been burned out yet. Hasn't been seen around. I'll bet he's staying close to home guarding what's his. He might know some more names, or we could leak his then wait and see what happens."

"What you reckon he'd say to leaking his? Makes fresh bait out of him."

She shrugged. "He's a pretty odd fella, but he isn't afraid of much. It'd be worth a try."

"Who is this man and where's his ranch?"

"Buck Dawson. He runs the Buckle D up on the Red River but west of here a ways. A day's ride anyway."

"First thing in the morning, I want to talk to Julio, see if we can borrow his deputy for the day. He's one heck of a tracker. Maybe we ought to deputize a couple more fellas to go along. If he says yes, we'll get out the word that we've found someone who's willing to give us names and set up a trap."

She tapped the table. "Dell, I never told you, but back when I was trailing this fella, I noted one of the shoes on his horse had a lightning strike crack through it. Made him easy to follow. I finally lost his trail over in Ojo. That's just so you can tell this trackin' fella. So, how do we put out the word?"

"I'll keep that in mind for Antonio. On setting up the trap, we'll send word to some people who like to talk. It'll get around fast. Maybe I could get it in the newspapers at Thomas City, Carlton, and Cactus Junction. Hawkins Post doesn't have one, but we could tell it around. Put up posters. It'll spread like wildfire once the right people hear about the big reward and such."

Brand spoke up. "Sounds like this could be a long, drawn-out affair."

"Probably. Why? You got a pressing date?"

Whit and Dutch thought that hilarious and laughed so loud everyone in the saloon hushed to look at them.

Dell leaned in over the table. "This might be a good place to start the rumor that we have a man ready to talk about the fires. Just talk loud enough for the next table to hear us."

Rose set down her beer. "Man, I'll have to get in on that. They've raised the reward to five thousand dollars. That's a high-dollar bounty. I know someone who will give us some names of those who rode with 'em and burned out Amos." She raised her voice just a bit. "Yeah, ole Buck's afraid he's gonna be next to be burned out, so he'll talk."

Dell grinned. "That's enough. We'd better get going. It's a long ride to the Buckle D ranch, and I want to get there before the word gets around."

Clearly, even though he spoke in a normal tone, a few men close by heard the conversation. Hopefully, it would be enough to get it started. If Amos heard, he'd hightail it up there to get rid of Buck Dawson.

Rose leaned across the table and spoke low. "I'll start the rumor mill working around the other saloons in town tonight. That'll get it spread soon enough. See you in the morning."

Rose didn't sleep much that night. They were starting what could cause a lot of trouble if it weren't controlled right. But something had to be done before this man decided to burn a whole town to the ground. She did her own bit of talking that morning before everyone gathered. Besides the saloons there was the blacksmith, the owner of the apothecary, a couple of ranchers coming through town. The news should soon spread like wildfire.

When everyone met outside of town, Dell took over as he was known to do. She didn't really mind. He was a smart man who could get right down to business when it was needed, and he was one of the few men she actually respected.

"I've had an idea. I'm thinking, if we split up, half ride over to Carlton, the other up to Thomas City with the news that we have a posse member ready to talk, then we can meet at Palo Duro canyon to get on out to this fella's ranch and be ready for whatever we've stirred up to happen. Remember don't say nothing about us setting a trap for Amos. That'd warn him off."

Everyone nodded except Rose. When she disagreed, she wasn't afraid to say so, even to Dell. "I think you're making a mistake not swinging through Cactus Junction. If he's apt to be anywhere it's there. Men like Amos crave excitement and crowds, and their newspaper has a bigger circulation. Let me go over there and take care of that, then join you at the canyon."

"I'm going with Rose," Whit said in a stern voice.

"Why? You think I need a chaperone?"

"No, I think you need someone to make sure you ain't doing this just so you'll get the bounty money. You accidentally run across news of this yahoo, you take off after him on your own and we lose him."

"Don't you dare accuse me of being untrustworthy. I've never gone behind anyone's back just to get a bounty. We get it with this plan, we split it."

Dell put up a hand. "No sense in getting in a big fight over this. There's merit in Rose's suggestion, but Whit has a point, too, on pairing up. However, I hate to bust your balloon, Whit, but as lawmen, we can't share in a bounty."

"Now, wait a minute," Rose shouted. "I can damn well take care of myself. Don't need no one tagging along."

Dell cut her off. "No, listen. Two together can get a lot more done and protect each other at the same time. This man doesn't care who he hurts or kills, and Rose has already been grabbed once for being involved. So, that's the way we'll do it. Rosie and Whit will go to Cactus Junction, Brand and Dutch will hit Carlton, and I'll go home to Thomas City where I'll deputize a couple of good men to come with me and meet y'all at the canyon. Then all of us will ride out to this ranch where we hope Amos will show up to set a fire. If he is indeed our arsonist, and if he gets wind of our planted rumor." He doubled his fist in anger. "Dammit, this is awful iffy to get so many involved, but it looks like the best chance we've got."

Rose didn't like it that Dell came out against her, but she kept her silence. Fighting never brought about anything but trouble, and they needed this to work. She didn't always have to have her way, though she liked it when she did.

With a shrug, she smiled an agreement toward Dell. "Long as ole Whit here understands we haven't time to gamble, it's do our job and get out."

"I know how to do my job. You keep quiet and don't nag, and we'll get along fine." Whit's face turned a fiery red.

"I wouldn't dream of it. We'd better get moving then. It's a good ride to Cactus Junction. Come on, Whit, move your ass."

After unloading their gear from the pack horse and tying it on their horses, she and Whit climbed in their saddles.

An echo of laughter followed her, and she goaded the prancing Andalusian into a dance just to show off. Behind her, came the sound of Whit's pony galloping to catch up. She did her own laughing then. No one could outdo Cimarron, and Whit was in for a challenge keeping up.

TWELVE

IN THE LATE AFTERNOON DELL returned home from Hawkins Post and rode directly to the barn out back where he took care of Curly's needs before hurrying to the house. Guinn met him on the front porch and went into his arms. After a kiss, she urged him to come inside where he kicked off his boots and followed her.

"I have a fresh pound cake just turned out of the pan with butter I churned this morning. You look tired."

"I'll admit that cake sounds and smells great after trail eating off and on."

Inside, the warmth and scent of baking wrapped around him. The woman sure could make him feel cared for. There was nothing like loving and being loved. If he hadn't found Guinn, he wouldn't be the man he was, well-fed and feeling special. The cake was sweet and so blamed tasty. Each bite was like getting an extra hug from Guinn. Her baking one of his favorite cakes soothed his aching soul. Recovering from such things as dealing with someone so mean spirited as to burn homes and families and a mercantile was hard. What would that terrible man do next if not stopped? The worst thing of all was he couldn't bear the idea of families burning to death.

At the table, Guinn spoke almost the same words. Fear colored the tone of her voice and the expression in her eyes. She was suffering from more than just this case.

Tears poured down her cheeks. "The children, heavens the children. How can anyone human do such evil things?" She covered her face with both hands and broke into racking sobs.

He rose and put his arms around her, holding her close. Her heart wrenching suffering hurt him in ways he couldn't express.

Losing their son—Teddy—to whooping cough at the age of two had almost killed Guinn and broke him for a long time. He had his work, but she could barely function for months afterward. It was understandable that she was so upset over Horner's acts she could hardly discuss it with him. It was best to change the subject before she broke down completely. Dang, if she fell into a deep sorrow over this, she might never recover.

Still sniffling she set the cake and a bowl of fresh butter down in front of him, and he covered her trembling hand with his. "It's going to be all right, sweetheart. I love you, you know, and we'll get through this, I promise."

She encircled his shoulders and held him close, her muscles trembling against him. Then she shook her head, took a deep breath and kissed him. "I'm okay. Please don't go off worrying about me. You need to be careful. This man is dangerous."

"I don't want you to think over-much about this fire starter coming back. I think he's made his statement here in Thomas City. And we're going to stop him. No one seems to think the boy had anything to do with the fire, though I'm pretty sure he's Amos Horner's son. I can't imagine one single family in Saddler County who doesn't care for their own better than that. The man is so cruel-hearted, he's thrown the boy away. Not feeding or clothing him properly is a disgrace. He'll pay for his sins. You wait and see. We have plans to trap him soon. I'm afraid, though, I will have to leave first thing tomorrow. We're riding up to the Red River where a man lives who was a part of that terrible posse. He may be the answer to trapping this evil so-and-so."

She dropped into the chair next to him, broke a bit off his piece of cake and held it as if afraid to enjoy the taste. "Will you be in danger, then, from this awful man?"

"Please don't worry, sweetheart. I can't think of you in such a state while I'm gone. Perhaps we should get someone to stay with you."

"Oh, no. I'm fine. Don't worry about me. Just take care of yourself."

"If you're sure. I'm taking several good men with me, so I'll be okay. Oh, and Rosie is meeting us."

"Oh, Rose, is it? Why doesn't she find a good man and settle down to having children? Bounty hunter, indeed. It's unsavory. I guess I understand a bit, since her mother was a victim, but even before that she wore britches and rode clothespin all over the west hunting down outlaws, of all things."

"Now, don't be too quick to judge Rosie and what she does. If I remember correctly, you were quite the wild girl when we first met. You were the young lady who won a turkey at the fair for your perfect sharpshooting."

"Yes, but I didn't carry that over to shooting men, now did I? Though heaven knows most of them deserve it." Eyes red from crying, she covered her mouth.

He patted her hand. "It's all right. No need to worry. But I know you like her. And it's no sin to admit it." He cut off a large bite of the butter-soaked cake and chewed it. His gaze caught hers. "I think you admire her get up and go without permission from anyone."

"Why, Dell Hoffman, I've never needed permission from any man, most especially you."

He tipped his head back and laughed but said nothing. A relief that she could joke overcame some of his concern about leaving her. She'd be fine, being the strong woman that she was.

"Okay, you're right, I do admire her courage, yes, indeed I do. Will she come for supper after this is over, do you think?"

He continued to smile. "So she can tell you of her latest adventures?"

She flushed, the color of her cheeks accenting her blue eyes and red hair. "Oh, shush, Dell. Look, the sun is setting. Rather than light the lamps, would you just as soon retire for the night?"

"That idea appeals to me. It sure is good to be home." He took the last bite of cake, stood, pulled her to her feet, and tilted her chin to give her a kiss on the mouth. "And that is just the beginning, my sweet."

"Well, then let's get to the middle." She took his hand and led him into the bedroom.

The next morning the scent of bacon frying brought Dell instantly awake. Dawn added the first rays of sunlight to the otherwise dim room, and he pawed at the pile of clothing on the floor, smiled at the memory of the previous night and slipped into his drawers. No more daydreaming. Time to get moving.

He paused to give Guinn a pat on the butt in the kitchen where the kettle steamed on the stove. Mixing hot water with a bit of cold, he stropped his straight razor a few times and shaved in front of the mirror hanging above the washpan in the corner.

Just as he came up from splashing his face, a man cleared his throat behind him and he jumped, turned to see Dutch palming a mug of coffee at the table. "Good morning, Sheriff. Thought you'd want an early start. Sorry I startled you. Your wife let me in. Go ahead with what you were doing."

Guinn laughed and placed two plates of eggs and bacon in front of the men.

"Aw, you don't have to feed me, Missus, but it sure looks good."

"Eat, the both of you. I'll set yours in the warming oven 'til you finish there, Dell." Her voice held a bit of merriment at their teasing.

"Shaving. I'm finished shaving. I was washing. Liked to drowned me, sneaking up on me like that." He dried his hands and face and rubbed his fingers over his smooth cheeks while looking in the mirror. Sometimes he left some brush here or there, but he didn't find any.

Dutch dug into his eggs. "Angelo's here. Boy is he one mean looking Apache. Said his cousin Julio over to Hawkins Post sent him to help us out.

Said it in about three words. Looking at him, I have no doubt but what he can throw two men over a barn. I sent him over to the café to get breakfast on our account. Hope that was okay. Oh, and there's a couple of men at the office wanting to see you."

"Good, I was expecting Angelo. Yes, it was a fine idea to feed him, though he'll eat a mighty heaping of food. Those other two fellas say what it's about?"

"Yeah, they heard the rumors about Horner, and they want to be part of our posse going to get this man."

"Oh, really? Who told them we're putting together a posse? That's not what's happening. What'd you tell them?"

"To wait there and you'd be in soon and they could talk to you. That's all I said."

Dell nodded. "Good." Satisfied with the job on his face, he went to the cook stove and took his plate from the warming oven. At the table, he sat and grabbed two biscuits, slathered them in fresh butter, and dug in.

Twenty minutes or so later, Dutch thanked Guinn for breakfast and went on back to the office to tell the men the sheriff was coming. Dell kissed her goodbye and went to the barn to saddle Curly. Both the men stood on the edge of the boardwalk waiting for him when he rode to the office. Dutch sat inside going through wanted posters delivered the day before while they were all out of town. Guy Goodson, the jailer, swept the jail floors, whistling a merry tune as he well might, always tending the jail while others went off to be shot at.

Before Dell could dismount, the men rushed out to greet him and started talking about riding with a posse.

"Is that the rumor that's going around town, that I'm getting up a posse to go after this man?"

Both said yes.

"Not quite true. No posse on this trip. I'm looking to deputize someone who can shoot and ride without trouble, who will do as they're told and aren't afraid of some dangerous work and hard riding and can be gone for a while. Could be a week or longer. Is that either one of you?"

The pair glared at each other, then back at Dell. Both were local. He'd seen them around, and vaguely knew who they were. The younger one went by the name of Gilbert Lincoln. He raised hay and sold it to ranchers and could probably be gone this time of the year. His fields would be up good. He'd do if he could be shot at without wetting his pants. The other though, had a steady job at one of the nearby ranches and they were way too busy to lose him— Moving cattle from winter pasture, culling out all the sick and injured, vaccinating, repairing fences. Hell, he could count the jobs off in his head. Harsh work. The fella probably imagined riding with Dell to be easier, but he was dead wrong. And Dell wasn't stealing a good hand.

So, he pointed at Lincoln, the farmer, who didn't look very old, though he appeared a bit weary. "You're not armed. Can you shoot?" Without waiting for an answer, he hollered. "Dutch bring me a rifle."

Dutch came out holding a Remington rolling block, handed it to Dell along with a cartridge. He grinned. So did Dell, before he led the man around behind the row of buildings on the main street where several targets were set up in an empty meadow. If this fellow could handle a rolling block with dexterity and hit a target, he'd do.

"They call me Gil," he offered and eyed the Remington.

"Can you load and shoot this?" Dell held out the single shot rifle along with one of the large metal cartridges.

Gil took the gun and cartridge. "Beautiful weapon." Stock tucked under his right arm he gauged the target, then raising the barrel, he thumbed back the hammer, then the breech lock, snapped the bullet in with his left hand, closed the breech lock, raised the rifle, aimed at the target and pulled the trigger, all in one smooth action. He didn't blink when the gun fired its heavy-throated boom.

Taking a deep breath, he glanced at Dell, "Want me to do it again?"

Dutch went to the target and pointed at dead center.

"Nah, that'll do. Good shooting. Where'd you learn?"

"In the war, but I didn't have one of these." His fingertips caressed the gleaming barrel.

"You must've been a kid. How'd you learn to handle it?"

"I was barely sixteen." He frowned and looked at the ground, then back up, his expression clearing. "Read up on it. Been saving for one, but …." He handed the rifle to Dell who gave it back to him.

"You'll do, son, you'll do. If you can leave in an hour. You'll carry this." He patted the Remington.

"Oh, I can leave now, sheriff."

He had his men, now to take care of this business, once and for all. He wouldn't come back 'til he did.

IT WAS MORE THAN ROSE could do to keep from laughing at Whit. He rode well, but riding an Indian paint was a challenge to the best of riders, and a day spent in that saddle gave anyone a sore butt.

She slowed Cimarron to allow him to catch up and, when he did, looked down from her saddle. "Why don't you get yourself a decent mount? Is it that they don't pay you enough as town marshal or what?"

"We're attached, ma'am, me and this sweet pony. He can't help he bumps a lot. We don't usually ride out much, just having town duties, but after all this riding I've about decided to do so. I've had Old Paint since I was even younger than fifteen and just can't seem to give him up."

"Well, you might put a collar on him, call him your pet dog and get something a bit closer to your size and job. Something that needs a saddle." She could barely keep from laughing just looking at the two of them. Whit was nearly six feet tall with long legs to match, but he was skin and bones, so he probably didn't stress the pony weight-wise. Looking at them, one might believe Whit could stand up straight and the pony walk out from under him.

"I guess you're right, but it won't do to have you make fun of us. Old Paint has his feelings hurt real bad."

"Just how old is that pony? You might need to put him out to pasture."

"I knew I hadn't ort to agreed to come to Cactus Junction with you. There are better ways I can spend my days than being made fun of by a woman bigger 'n me and prob'ly meaner, too. And I know Old Paint don't 'preciate it."

"We're coming up on the town, so I'll hush up, but would you ride in a few paces behind me, so folks don't know we're together?"

"Now you gone and made me mad enough to do just that. And when some yahoo rides off with you over his shoulder, I'll just sit and watch."

"Sit and watch this." She touched one heel against Cimarron's side and the smooth riding horse began a sideways prance down the center of the street. People stopped on both sides of the boardwalk to admire the performing Andalusian.

When she tied up in front of the Rocking Horse Saloon, Whit approached, stepped down, and tied his pony. "Choose this place for any specific reason? Like making more fun of my horse?

"For your information, I think I want one of those." He held a palm up to Cimarron and the dun snuffled and rolled his lip, then tossed his head. Whit laughed. "He agrees. I'll just take him home with me."

Whenever anyone admired her horse, it touched a well-hidden soft spot in her heart. She cleared her throat. "Well, let's get inside and begin our act. Remember, all we need to do is start a rumor that Buck Delaney is about to reveal the name of the men in the posse to trick Amos into picking him for the next ranch to burn, nothing more or less. Soon enough it ought to get around to Amos's ears. I sure hope this works."

"Reckon we ort to watch each other to make sure he don't decide to take a shot at one of us."

"Yep, he's killed that way before down in Lubbock or Amarillo, or both I reckon, so we need to be careful. You ready?"

She shot one last glance at Whit, and they went inside. Hopefully, he could stop any attempt on either of their lives. She'd better hope she could do the same, 'cause this was dangerous work they were doing. Not quite like when she hunted killers. This time, one was apt to be hunting them once the word got around town.

They were in the third saloon called Muddy Creek, her with her back to the wall chatting with a couple of friendly men who'd bought her a drink, claiming they did so even if she did wear britches, and Whit was at a table playing Twenty-One. She took a sip of whiskey after one of the men said something about the burning of the ranches.

Eyeing him flirtatiously she tilted her head. "Me and some others are on our way to talk to a rancher who knows the identity of the man who's doing it."

One of the men grimaced from a long gulp of whiskey, set down his glass and stared hard at her. "What then, you gonna magically find this fella? Guarantee you he's hid out good and no one's ever gonna find him."

She shrugged, not wanting to reveal any more about their plans to trap Horner. "Yes, but we're going to learn who all rode in the posse, too. Warn them he's coming."

After all her promises, Amos wouldn't be the only man ready to shoot her and Whit. Maybe those men in the posse wouldn't want their names bandied around either.

Still, they might need to know this fella was coming to burn them out. Wonder if it occurred to Dell or anyone else that this could go south on them real fast if it backfired? The remaining members of the posse could go to prison if the law so desired to charge them. They had murdered Horner's wife and baby.

Good Lord, what a mess. She had no idea what to say next. Both men were stunned into silence by what she told them. Maybe this wasn't something she should take part in. It could get everyone involved killed. And worse, what could she do about it now?

Ride off in the opposite direction, that's what. Find someone else to collect bounty on. There were plenty out there to choose from. But walk off and desert Dell? She'd never done something like that before.

She finished her drink, stood, thanked the men and, carrying her hat, meandered over to the table where Whit was winning then losing and signaled for his attention. Just as he looked up, one of the men she'd been drinking with came up behind her and clamped her wrist hard.

"We want to talk to you outside, if you don't mind."

"Afraid I do." With a quick twist she hammered his own fist into his stomach and put her knee between his legs. He doubled over, howled and went down. The other one reached for her, but Whit was there so fast she didn't see him move. He had the man on the floor, sitting astride him with both thumbs in his eyes. Afraid her man would get up she tackled him and was whipping him across the face with her Stetson when someone grabbed her arms and pulled her to her feet.

"Don't you know it's not good manners for a lady to beat up a gentleman."

She stared the man down. Actually, he was several inches shorter than her, so he was already looking up. "Well, he's no gentleman. They started it. We just finished it."

Another man rushed over and both displayed a badge on their vests.

Definitely wouldn't be good for them to go to jail, so she smiled and introduced Whit as the town marshal of Thomas City. "We're on our way to meet Sheriff Dell Hoffman. We're going to check on a report that the escaped killer, Amos Horner, has been spotted, and we're headed that way."

"Well, lady, I'm afraid you're gonna be just a little late." The sheriff handcuffed her, and the one on the floor was released to cuff Whit.

Rose had crossed paths with almost every lawman in the panhandle, and then some, but she had never met these two who arrested her and Whit and tossed them in jail for fighting in a saloon. Then the idjits let the ruffians go who started it. Also, she could claim loud and clear that one did not argue with a lawman even when he so obviously was a class A number one fool.

So, the next best thing was to either plead ignorance or flat out lie about motivation for your actions. The only reason it might be against the law to fight back when hit was, she picked the wrong person to knee in the balls. The fellow who started the fight hadn't been arrested or even scolded for being a bad boy. Maybe, they thought he'd had punishment enough, but she doubted it, though he was sort of pale.

Either way, she had to give it a try. She and Whit were wanted at Palo Duro Canyon by another sheriff, but she could hardly tell this lawman that. He'd want to set out with a posse, which had started all the problems to begin with.

She looked down into the marshal's inquisitive stare and gave it a try. "This is Marshal Whit Burns out of Thomas City, and I'm an undercover Pinkerton agent. We're after Amos Horner who is wanted for several recent murders. But it's a secret mission. He can't get word he's being pursued." She poked Whit. "Show him your badge. I don't carry one because it's dangerous should I get caught by this Horner."

Whit looked from her to the extremely short marshal, fumbled around 'til he dug out his badge that he carried in a pocket.

Marshal Hunter, who compensated for his height with high-heeled boots, gazed up through the cell bars into her serious features with a look of total disbelief, then inspected Whit's badge.

"Looks fake to me. Who do you work with up there in Thomas City? And why is it a secret?"

"Sheriff Dell Hoffman, but I'm the town marshal. Assigned—" he cut his gaze toward Rose as if he'd rather crawl in a hole than do this. "—to help—uh—agent—"

She butted in. "He doesn't know my real name, and I won't reveal it to you. But I will tell the rangers who cautioned us not to tell a living soul, how

much you assisted in seeing we could pursue a hot lead on where this Horner is hiding out without any interference. I was you, I wouldn't want those
rangers down on me. We have to get after him soon as we can. It's of the
utmost importance. He's a menace to the entire panhandle, to all of Texas,
maybe to the entire country. I'm sure you understand the need for secrecy."

The expression on Hunter's face was one of excitement and a hot desire
to be a part of such a pursuit.

Thirty minutes later they fled the confines of the Cactus Junction jail that
held a furious marshal behind bars. Riding hell for leather they left the city
limits behind, Whit laughing so hard he could hardly remain on his pony.

THIRTEEN

A BRUTAL COLD WIND WHIPPED Dell's coat against his chaps, a slapping noise that spooked Curly. He rubbed the horse's neck with gloved hands and spoke to him in soft tones. Just like the Texas panhandle weather to go from balmy spring to end of winter. And them, headed north. Next, it'd be ice pellets. Lowering his head for protection beneath the brim of his Stetson, he pushed on. Muted clopping assured him that Dutch and newly-deputized Gil Lincoln rode at his flank. Turning his head to check would mean a gust square in the face, so he didn't.

In his mind, he lined out the plans for this manhunt to trap Amos Horner. His deputy, Brand, was on his way to Hawkins Post to fetch Angelo. Marshal Julio Jenkins had offered his cousin, the full blood Apache, to go with them as tracker. Rose and Whit would meet them at Palo Duro. If all went as planned the six of them would go up against the killer, Amos Horner, hopefully at Buck Dawson's ranch. Anything could go wrong with his plans, the worst being someone could get shot. Best not to think of that.

What if some of the other members of that dreadful posse decided to stop Dawson from revealing all their names? Ending Amos's unholy acts of revenge was really only a part of Dell's plan. If this didn't work Amos would still be on the loose and a danger to the families of the remaining few members. He wouldn't give up though. It was a complicated plan and could go awry easily.

They had to stop Amos at the Buckle D Ranch, no two ways about it. What the law had in mind for the posse members who had committed their own heinous acts remained unknown. Some of them had already paid the ultimate price.

Dutch caught up with him. "Hope this weather blows by." Some of the shouted words were blown away.

"Maybe down in the canyon the wind'll lay."

The deputy rode along in silence. He must want to say something, and Dell had a feeling he knew what.

"Boss, what if this bastard gets away from us, or he don't even try to burn the Buckle D? He might head for one of the other ranchers on his list." He shouted as if the question had to be said despite the circumstances.

Dust, dirt, and grit filled the air and stung any skin exposed. Dell hunkered inside the rain gear as much as he could, pulled his bandana up over his nose and trusted Gil and Dutch had done the same, so he didn't attempt to reply to the question.

Someone hailed them, voice carrying with the wind. Coming from the North.

He reined up, turned Curly's butt to the wind and pulled down the bandana. "Hold up. Someone's coming. Might be Brand and that Apache. Can't see nothing in this storm."

Two riders appeared almost as if blown in by the wind. "It's us, Boss. Didn't know if we'd find you. This Apache's a wonder. I'd swear you could blindfold him, and he'd find his way home or wherever. We left out last night, come most of the trip in the black of night except for some cloud shine. Danged if I wouldn't welcome some shelter about now."

At long last they'd reached the trail down into the canyon. The weak sun had crossed the sky to mark most of a day riding and hung what looked like inches above the horizon. Weary to the bone, Dell dismounted a like-wise worn-out Curly. The gelding gave a grunt as if he were dead on his feet. Dang, he hated to ride a horse like that.

"Let's get down to the bottom before dark. Gil, we'll have to dismount and lead the animals."

"Sure, glad we're gonna stay here all night." Gil swung out of the saddle and wrapped the reins around one hand.

Dutch turned his back to the wind to survey the countryside. "Reckon Rose and them's already here?"

"We get to the bottom we'll talk about what's next. Come on, it's too blamed windy and cold to stand here palavering." Dell led the way, while behind him, horses' hooves kicked up loose gravel that clattered into the tops of trees far below, an unfortunate warning to any outlaws hid out below.

The deeper they went, the better the weather, as if the great walls of the canyon offered soothing arms. Relieved, Dell raised his head from its tilted position and kept an eye out ahead of them. Since outlaws used the canyon frequently for a hideout, it was apt to be a welcome shelter for many to-night. He sure didn't want to get shot.

"Be wary. Guards are out who might take potshots at anyone who comes too close to their camp. Don't return fire, just hide."

Dutch chuckled low.

Glad of the man's sense of humor, Dell grinned. He was only after two outlaws this trip, the others could well feel safe, but sometimes it was hard to put that across to some lawmen.

Actually, he hoped to run into Jake and his bunch. Often, they heard mutterings from others and would share with him, being the sort they were, and him being the sort he was. He tended to leave them be as well, though that wasn't something he'd admit.

There were down and dirty outlaws, and then there were those work-ing on the boundaries, trying to make things right that the war had ru-ined as best they could. Those folk left poor by battles benefited from their spoils, most of which came from carpetbaggers, usury bankers and the like. Then there were the no-goods who profited from thefts much worse than Jake's bunch, then hid behind the law.

It was dark in the bottom of the canyon, the only light that from the clouds in the sky that reflected an eerie unexplainable light. The line of men cast vague wavy shadows on the canyon bluffs as they descended. At the bottom the horses picked their way, easily guided to a cutback in the high walls that formed a shelter against both rain and wind. Dell halted and leaned against Curly to take some deep breaths. It'd been a long hard day.

"This'll do for the night. We can hear anyone coming down the trail and spot them through that crevice yonder while we wait for the others to join us. We'll trade off keeping watch in case Rose rides through the night or some no good decides to sneak up on us."

"Boss, let me ride out that direction and check on Rose and Whit. She's a good hand at keeping at it. Something must've happened to them." Dutch had one foot in the stirrup ready to mount if Dell okayed it.

Above, the howling of the wind made the only sound while Dell stared out into space considering. that Dutch was probably right, but if none came back, then he was short three hands. And he needed them all if they were going to successfully ambush Horner. "Tell you what. Ride out maybe an hour in that direction, no more. Come on back if you don't find them. I just can't chance losing all of you to some crazed outlaw running the trail in this storm. Some of 'em shoot anything that moves or kill for a man's horse."

Dutch agreed and took off, his path marked by the tumbling of rocks from under the horse's hooves.

Once everything was unloaded, Gil and Brand went about gathering deadwood while Dell filled the coffeepot with water and laid out their bed-rolls. Angelo disappeared without a word. Probably checking out their surroundings. He could sneak up on the wariest of men without being heard or seen. It was easy to forget he even rode with them. Soon they had a fire crackling, food put out, and coffee brewing.

"I think it's warm enough to hang our wet things to dry without freezing. Funny how wind makes such a difference." Dell draped his rain gear, jacket, and gloves over some bushes near the fire. Gil and Brand did the same. The flames put out warmth that felt good.

"Or maybe it's no wind that makes the real difference," Gil added.

They relaxed around the fire, drinking strong black coffee and eating Guinn's delicious baking.

Angelo returned and said nothing. He hadn't spoken one word since joining them. He accepted a share of the baked goods with only a nod, as if he didn't speak or understand much English. He could fool most everyone that way. Tricky fella.

According to Julio the large Apache had been with those who refused to surrender when that dwindling tribe was given a choice by the white man. Surrender and go to the reservation or be sent away to prison. When imprisonment was threatened, some of those accustomed to riding free, hunting buffalo, and pulling their raids on other tribes, hid out in Texas on land given to them by the Spanish in the early 1700s, rather than be submitted to the rules of a reservation. Others like Julio and Angelo took Spanish names and lived their lives quietly obeying the white man's law. They spoke a mixture of Spanish, Apache and English.

"Your wife packs some tasty fixins," Gil said. "I met her once in town. Helped her carry some goods to her wagon. Nice lady."

"Yep, she is that. Thank you. I'll tell her you enjoyed her cake. You married, Gil?"

"Was once. She died while I was away in the war. I've never took the time to look around for anyone since. Just can't imagine replacing my lovely Amy." His voice cracked but he went on. "I admit I miss having the woman's touch around the house. Nothing like doing your own laundry and cooking to make you appreciate that."

"You're wise not to marry just for a cook and laundress, though. That seldom works out. Marry for love. There's nothing like true love with a faithful woman. Took me time to find one, but once I did, I can't see getting along sleeping alone. Be good to a woman, be true and faithful and she'll bring you nothing but happiness and contentment. If you don't want no woman telling you what to do or how to do it, why then, don't boss her around, either." Dell looked into the fire for a minute or two, then continued.

"I don't know what I'd do without Guinn. She's the center of my life, but then she ain't one to tell a feller what to do, how or when to do it. She is good at making gentle suggestions though."

"My Amy was like that. Lord, I still miss her. Holding her in my arms, touching the back of her neck while she stood at the cook stove, the warm feel of her skin." His voice faded and none of them spoke for some time.

Finally, Dell rose. "Reckon I'll go drain the pickle and retire. Don't look like our companions will arrive tonight. Hope everything's okay with them. We need to get this done before more ranches burn."

Angelo rose, towering over them. "I will watch. You sleep." With that he found a comfortable boulder, leaned up against it, and said no more.

Dell grinned at the stoic reserve of the Apache, who was willing to help them out without question just because his uncle asked.

Stillness fell over the night like a soft blanket. A few serenading birds broke the silence calling to each other. The fire crackled and sent up fragrant smoke. The horses tied to a line shuffled and snuffled in their sleep. No one came down the trail. Dell was accustomed to sleeping light and could hear a pebble roll along the ground even when he was snoring in his bedroll. But the night passed, and no one came. Dang, what could've happened to all three of his missing hands?

Early the next morning, birds tuned up in the early light, then gleefully sang their songs to welcome the warmth of the sun. Gil proved his worth by starting an early fire and beginning a pot of coffee. Sometime during the night, he had changed places with Angelo keeping watch. They chewed on jerky for breakfast, Dell finishing first.

"We need to go find Brand, and Rose and Whit, Boss?"

"I think so. Anyways, ride out a few miles. We meet up with Rosie and Whit who'll cut our path about halfway to Carlton, then we'll decide our next move. I don't want to delay getting to the Buckle D, but we need those three to accomplish much."

Angelo rose to his full height. He touched his chest, pointed to his horse. "I could find. *Paseo rapido.*"

"Did he say he runs fast?" Gil asked.

"Actually, he said ride fast and indicated himself. Probably speaks mostly Apache but has learned a little English and Spanish just to get along." Dell cleared his throat. "I'd guess he understands most of what we say, though."

Angelo nodded vigorously and headed for his trim ash-colored mustang, clearly built to run as was the Apache built to ride.

Gil sprang to his feet. "I'll go with him. He might not come back, knowing what we're up to."

Dutch sprang to his feet, as if to make the same offer. Dell signaled them both back. "They'll all be here soon. We can trust the Apache. Meanwhile, let's see if Jake is here. He gets around, and he'll know what's going on around us."

He dragged his saddle from where he'd slept and tossed it on Curly. "Keep the campfire going. I'll ride around and see if I can find him. The canyon's a big place, but there is a huge ranch here. Charlie Goodnight acquired thousands of acres here in the canyon. It's a ways from us here, so we shouldn't have to worry about running across any of his hired men and getting shot at for trespassing. Just a word to the wise, though. I'm gonna take a look around." He bent to tie the latigo strap and there came the sound of approaching horse's hooves on the south trail. He mounted and went to investigate.

Sure enough, it was Brand.

Brand greeted him, keeping his voice low. "Hey there, Sheriff. Good to see you. I didn't see hide nor hair of Rose and Whit. Didn't go clear back to Cactus Junction. Something must've happened to 'em there is all I can figure."

Dell shook his head and frowned. Everyone nodded at each other.

"Well, there's nothing for it but to forge on. I'm going to see if Jake's gang is back in here somewhere. Brand, get yourself something to eat there. I think we left a few bites. I have something I want to talk to Jake about. Then, I reckon we might as well be on our way. We can't wait any longer for those two. They probably got hung up at one of the gambling tables."

He might've said that, but he didn't believe it for one minute. Rose was too dependable, even if he wasn't sure about Marshal Whit Burns. Something had happened, but he needed to get everyone on up to the Double D and stop this fire starter, if at all possible.

The large Apache sat on his haunches near the fire rubbing huge hands together and saying nothing.

Dell rode slowly among the rocks and crevices where most outlaws laid up occasionally. He was taking a chance on getting shot at. He was close to Jake's favorite hangout in the canyon when he was spotted by a guard. Hands held away from his gun, he introduced himself.

"Need to see Jake. It's really important."

"Wait here just a minute, Sheriff Hoffman."

Jake strolled out in a few minutes tucking his undershirt in his pants. "Come to arrest me this morning, Sheriff?" He grinned the joke up at Dell, palm curled around his six-shooter like he wasn't sure.

Dell wouldn't walk out of there alive if Jake so chose, but a certain trust existed between the two men because of Rosie.

"Why, you been up to no good?"

"Depends on who you ask."

"Nah, tell you what, and I don't want it to get around now. I'm headed for the Buckle D. Have you heard any tales about this Amos Horner, the man we're pretty sure is burning all the ranches?"

The palm of Jake's hand uncurled. "Heard about that. If I could get ahold of him, he'd be hanging from the nearest tree, but then you might not appreciate that. What would make a man do such a thing?"

"You might say he's grief struck." He told Jake the story of Horner and his own loss. "Still don't give him rights to do what he's doing."

"I might've gone out on a toot and shot me some men, but not helpless families asleep in their beds. That's not right, just not right." Jake stared off out across the canyon.

Dell nodded in agreement. "Any new gang members you're suspicious of maybe? I'm not trying to get any of your men in trouble, just looking hard to stop this uncalled-for killing."

"Normally, I wouldn't talk to the law about such men, but this one has me worried. Some of the things I heard him talking about …well, I just won't allow in my bunch. He claimed he was hiding out from some real bad yokels, so I let him stay. But after a day or two his wild talk bothered me, so I run him off. Name of Carl Iverson, and he had a young friend, Jimmy, with him. He just got too vicious in his ideas for what we ought to do, so I sent him packing here just a couple nights ago."

The back of Dell's neck crawled, and the hairs raised. "What'd he act like? I don't know what this feller looks like, but I got a hunch how he'd act. You have to be mad dog crazy to do what he's doing, and it would show. He couldn't help letting it. Truth be known, I'd like to see the whole posse locked up, but this …no."

"I agree, and this could well have been your man. Worse than that. That crazy Rafe Malone run with us a few days. He took up with this Carl and they left together. If I was Sheriff, I'd have 'em both in a cell buried so deep they'd never get out."

"Did they say anything about where they might be headed?"

"No, sorry to say. Spoke of maybe going down to Cactus Junction and doing some gambling. Then Iverson, he brought up some unfinished business he had to tend to, but said it could wait, it wasn't going nowhere. That owl-hoot, Rafe, agreed to help him with it. So no, nowhere specific."

"And the boy. What was he like? They say Horner's son escaped with him when that posse burned him out."

"The boy, I don't know about. He was a quiet one. Looked scared and hungry, too."

"They crazy enough to burn folks alive?"

"It wouldn't surprise me none since you mention it. But I would never believe any human could do such a thing. Say, you need some help corralling these sons of bitches some of my men'd be glad to help with that. Me, too."

"Thanks, Jake, but I need to keep it small and quiet. Appreciate your help. Oh, if you happen to see Rosie, tell her we're just over yonder for another hour or so." He pointed toward their camp.

Jake nodded. "Will do. So, she's throwed in on this with you? She's a fine one, that gal. Don't get her hurt."

Dell raised a goodbye wave without replying. He wasn't sure he could keep anyone from getting hurt on this ride. He sure wasn't.

ONCE CLEAR OF THE TOWN'S view, Rose slowed Cimarron to allow Whit to catch up. "I can't believe you pulled that off. No one else in the world could convince that marshal you're a Pinkerton agent. And further that when we catch Amos, you'll give Hunter credit for helping even though you locked him up."

"Me? *Me?* All I did was convince him he had to act like we overpowered him, so he wouldn't get in trouble. By the way, how could anyone believe someone riding a pinto pony could be the marshal of anything? I'm gonna buy you a decent mount at the very next ranch we come to where good horses can be found. I can't bear to watch you ride that poor pony another foot."

"Hey, don't talk bad about my horse. How'd you get him to believe such an outrageous story?"

"I'm just a very good liar, so be careful what you believe I say. Now, we'd better get ourselves down to the canyon before Sheriff Hoffman gives up and goes in after Amos alone."

The day was the exact opposite of the day before. The storm had passed on leaving behind rain-washed skies, trees, and bluffs. The wet ground smelled fresh and clean, and Rose continued to ride out in front of Whit. It couldn't be far to the canyon, but they should meet up with Dell and them before they had to start down. He wanted to ride out for the Buckle D first thing this morning.

"You know, Whit, I'm thinking we'll just wait at the rim of the canyon for them. It'd be sort of dangerous to meet them on the trail while we were going down and they were coming up."

Soon, low conversations rose up from below and Dell came into view followed by Brand, Dutch and a stranger she didn't know, Angelo and Jake, all leading their horses. Since the climb was muddy from yesterday's rain it wasn't safe coming or going.

Dell's eyes lit and his face changed from furrowed to wrinkled with pleasure. "It's sure good to see you both. We were worried about you."

Rose laughed. "If you knew what troubles we ran into, you'd know why we were late. Tell you all about it after we get underway. Hey there, Jake. Good to see you've joined us. That Horner's giving the rest of you outlaws a bad name, huh?" She smiled at Gil. "And who might you be? Some stray our sheriff picked up along the trail?"

Dell spurred Curly to ride alongside her. "We have our stories to tell as well, Rose, but you first. You get in trouble in Cactus Junction?"

"Things are run real odd there. It's like certain men are in charge of what goes on, and it's not the sheriff or town marshal." She told about their arrest for defending themselves in the saloon fight, and how they'd been arrested and put in jail while the others who started the fight went free.

"I don't get down that way too often," Dell said. "So, I don't know their sheriff or town marshal, but I'm sorry to hear something like that about any lawmen anywhere in Texas.

"Well, something ought to be done. The money flows 'cause of all the gambling, and I'd bet those two are getting more than their share of it."

Jake, who was riding just behind them spoke up. "Sounds like something I could take a hand in. Relieve them of some of the flowing money and put it where it'd do the most good."

"Don't be doing any talking about breaking the law in front of me, Jake or I'll have to send you back to your cave."

Jake laughed, and the others joined in. Everyone living in the panhandle knew about Jake and his need to see a redistribution of the wealth there. It was a well-known, poorly-kept, secret, no matter how you looked at it. That he actually saw to getting it done was not so well-known.

Rose feared that, one day, his checkered past would catch up with him, and some bounty hunter or strait-laced lawman would haul his head in for the reward money.

But that was in the future. Right now, they were all set on one goal, to cut down Amos Horner. And it would be more to be an end to his murdering than for the reward money. One or more of them probably wouldn't make it back, but like all who enforced the law out here in the panhandle, that was the least of any of their worries.

Rose dropped back to watch the riders as they kicked their mounts into a lope and headed out across the plains. Cimarron reared and she let out a shout, then took up the rear as if driving them on.

FOURTEEN

ONCE SPREAD OUT AND SETTLED into a comfortable riding formation, Dell had time to ruminate. How, for some reason, the arrival of the lovely Rosie lent a new mood to the entire gang. He'd often noticed the same thing in the presence of Guinn. Maybe women sent out a sweet fragrance, or perhaps it was the soft sound of their words, or they just walked different, but anyway, Dell had perked up when he heard Rose's voice. How he'd worried that something had happened to her. If it had, it would forever be his fault, allowing her to join them in this awful manhunt.

He chuckled to himself. He couldn't have stopped her, for she'd have gone in search for the fire starter on her own whether or not he'd let her ride with them. Still, he would be responsible if something happened to her. It had nothing to do with love. He loved Guinn with all his heart. This was admiration and appreciation of a beautiful woman. He wasn't sure how to explain it to himself. Right now, though, he didn't have time to explain anything. It would take his total attention to keep all of them safe from the maniacs they pursued. Adding Rafe Malone to the mix made Amos all that much more dangerous.

Thinking of Rosie must've called out to her, for she caught up with him on that beautiful bay horse of hers, both a picture of the true west if ever anything was. A woman in britches, silken blouse, and a Stetson. Boots to match the outfit. And her a bounty hunter. The only woman he held above her in his heart was Guinn.

"Good you're here, Rosie. We were getting worried."

She hooked a thumb over her shoulder toward Whit bringing up the rear on his plodding pinto. "It's him and that blamed pony that slowed us down. You've got to see your town marshal has a better mount or I will. My fault we got put in jail, but all the same, he slowed us down."

Her story of the experience in Cactus Junction and her and Whit escaping jail had both amused and annoyed him, not at her but at that pigheaded marshal. As long as she was safe, only this manhunt mattered. "It's a long way up to the Buckle D. You'll both have time to hash and rehash your stories. According to Jake, Rafe Malone may have hooked up with the fire starter. He says they left out a couple days ago for Cactus Junction. You didn't happen to run into them down there?"

"Nope. If I did, we wouldn't have to be riding after them now. I'd a laid out for them outside of town and shot them both down. "

"Then you would be in jail, and probably hung."

She laughed. "You're right. I thought we were going to get hung after I kicked that old boy in the balls." Dell burst out laughing and she went on. "They were the only ones we ran into. The two fellas in the saloon we tussled with and that blamed bunch of crooked lawmen."

She was silent for a while. He glanced at her, and she met his gaze.

"I guess I ought to've killed Rafe when I got the chance. By now, he's probably learned how to fire a gun with his left hand. I'll take care of that when I see him."

"From what Jake said, those two will be up to a lot of mischief along the way, so we have to think they don't know about our plans for Buck Dawson's place."

Dell considered his crew of six men and one woman who rode now in silence, perhaps contemplating what lay ahead. They were an odd bunch, but each one could be counted on to do what was necessary. He just hoped to God killing wouldn't be on the list, but it was better than getting killed, any day of the week. Having an outlaw, a bounty hunter, a farmer, an Apache and three lawmen come together for one good cause might be a first. It sure didn't hurt to have one of the best gun hands in Texas along. Jake could be trusted to do what was right on either side. This might call for unexpected actions, though his hope was to take Amos Horner alive, if at all possible. Rafe Malone he could expect to resist.

Behind him, his special posse rode across the open plains, pacing the horses to put the fastest miles behind them without harming the animals. Out here in the open anyone was a target.

Dell had finally told them to spread out, making separate targets. Because she'd ridden this country a lot, Rose rode ahead to play scout and Whit went with her, like they had become pals or something. Dell preferred a long line, so the group didn't make a good target. It wasn't even an hour or so later when he heard the pounding of hooves and a hollering.

He cut out of line to meet Rose coming back full tilt on that beautiful dun. She hauled up and pointed off to the southwest. "Look, yonder."

A spiral of ashen gray smoke rose into the blue sky, a high wind scattering it.

"Hold up a minute. That's down toward Carlton."

"What do you think, Sheriff?"

"Damn, is what I think, Brand. Several small farms down there. Only one ranch of any size. A family owns it. The Braxtons—and they've got kids."

Cimarron pranced and Rose held him with a word. "Want me to go? I can get there and be back in no time. If they need help—"

Jake reined out of line to join them. "Looks like a building burning. Not trees or a grass fire. Smoke's the wrong color."

"What do you want to do, Boss?" The first time the new deputy, Gil, had put in a word.

Dell studied each one of his crew. Had Horner decided to stop and set a fire just for the hell of it, or was this one of the ranchers who'd ridden in the posse and helped kill the man's family? He had no idea. Worse, why did it matter to the decision he made? Antonio sat his gray, the horse as nervous as his rider to be the one to go, but he waited for Dell to give an order.

Gil spoke up again. "I'll go. I know that family and most of the folks over there. I'll help where I can then catch up with you. I also know where the Buckle D is."

Dang, he hated this, but something had to be done. He stared at the pillar of smoke rising into the windless air. Nodded. "Okay, Gil. Trade horses there if you can then ride hell bent to catch us. Even with Jake, I'm satisfied I'm gonna need you one and all, what with Rafe being added to the brew."

Gil turned his mount.

Dell called out. "And don't mention us at all, just get back to us soon as you can get away. I have a hunch that bastard likes to watch his handiwork from a close distance."

The small posse waited in silence for Dell to do something. He waved his hat. "Well, let's get underway."

They went back to their long line, each rider matching his horse's trot to the others. Only Cimarron occasionally danced or broke trot to show off his abilities. Dell had to wonder where someone had come across such a magnificent animal, and how they had managed to give it away. Obviously, whoever it was thought an awful lot of Rosie to make such a gift.

Riding across the panhandle allowed a fella a lot of uninterrupted time to think. Time to see forever. And out there in forever appeared a speck, something that didn't belong. He kept a wary eye on it 'til it grew in size. A bush or tree? It was off to one side of them, so its movement became apparent, so it was not standing still. He strained to make out a shape or size, and as it came closer it was evidently a galloping horse. What made it look so strange was something dangling along one side. Bouncing.

Dear God, it was a rider, leg hung in a stirrup. The horse, a black almost as big as Cimarron, was terrified out of its mind. The whites of his eyes gleamed. Coming right toward them kicking up great clods of grass. Would anything stop him?

BEHIND ROSE, DELL YELLED SO loud she whirled the bay, who could turn on a two-bit piece, and spotted the problem. She dug her knees in, leaned forward along Cimarron's neck and headed for the runaway horse.

He was going to run Whit down. Whit froze with his pinto right in the stampeding animal's way.

"Turn him, turn him." The plea whispered in Cimarron's ear was all it took. He rounded the black up as if it were a stampeding herd. Dust and clods flew from under scrambling hooves, the horses screamed. Her knees rubbed against the black's shoulders, close to being crushed. Cimarron shifted, turned neck to neck alongside the terrified horse. Rose flattened along his straining muscles. Smelled the sweat of horseflesh. Released the reins so the bay did what he instinctively knew to do. Turned the other horse. When both animals hauled to a stop, she held their reins in gloved hands, the black snorting, sweat pouring from under its saddle and foaming over the ebony coat.

She reached out and rubbed between laid-back ears. "Hush now, hush. You're okay." The amazing bay holding in place as if its rider had done nothing more than lasso a calf and tie its legs. The black stood splayed legged, each breath loud in the noonday heat.

All six riders were gathered closely by the time she brought the horse under control.

Angelo, who seldom spoke, said clearly, "She ride like Apache."

No one seemed to know what else to say or do, or if they did know they couldn't voice it.

At last she swung off Cimarron, rubbed his shoulder then that of the black. "Someone come get this body loose. Come on, it's safe." Was she going to have to do that herself?

A groan came from the unfortunate fella. He wasn't dead but hung tight in the stirrup.

"He's alive, help me get him loose." She went to her knees.

Blood covered his face and hands, his clothing, especially his britches, was ripped revealing torn flesh on both legs.

Dell knelt beside her and went to work getting the bent leg untangled. The man shouted with pain when his limp foot fell to the ground.

"It's broken. Good Lord, who would do this to someone?"

The terrified Whit, who had managed to slide off his pinto, looked as frightened as if he were still in danger. "Maybe he just fell off and got caught. These big horses can hurt you bad without any help."

Surprised by the weak tone of Whit's voice, Rose glanced his way. That's why he rode that docile small paint. He was afraid of horses. Strange for most living in the west, but from his accent he came from the east. Maybe he'd never ridden before.

Rose gently examined the rider's wounds. "Dell, we have to get him help."

"I know, but I can't spare any more of you. We have to stop Horner, no matter what."

She lay a hand on his arm, "If this were me looking like this, would you just ride off and leave me?"

"Of course not, but he may have committed a robbery or shot someone. Why else would he be fleeing across the panhandle like the devil himself were after him?"

"I can take him." Whit's gentle voice broke into their conversation. "I'm really no use to you out at the Buckle D. I'm not a lawman, I worked in Philadelphia for an attorney. I came west to be a cowboy, never realizing it would be—" he gestured around "—like this. I'll flat-out admit I'm scared. I can't go any further with you. Put him on my pony and I'll take him to the nearest house."

"Whit, how will you know where that is?"

"What could be so hard about that? You can see a hundred miles in this godforsaken country. I'm going to pack up and go back to Philly, I'm not cut out for this kind of shit."

Rose laughed and everyone joined her. Whit had never used such a word before. It relieved the tension somewhat.

Jake, who had remained removed from the fracas 'til now, wandered over. "That black is tamed down now, why don't you ride him and haul this fella on yours, or the other way around?"

Whit shook his head fiercely. "No sir, I won't take that big black into my care. He wants to run, he'd run, and I couldn't stop him either. I prefer to walk any day."

There was no arguing with him, so they boosted the injured man stomach-down across the back of the pony, that being the only way he'd stay on.

She shook hands with Whit like a man to man and thanked him. "I reckon you won't be wanting me to get you that horse after all."

He grinned, half shame faced. "Think I'll just keep old pinto here. Have to admit I bought him soon as I got off the train from Philadelphia. Never owned a pony in my life. Sorry I lied."

Dell came over and shook his hand. "You take care now and stay out of the way of any yahoos. Find a way to let us know where you go, would you?"

Rose admired Dell for treating the small man with respect. It was another reason she held the sheriff in such esteem, the way he never put down anybody except maybe the meanest of outlaws.

Whit walked off in the direction Dell suggested, explaining there were some farmers down that way who would take in the injured man. Rose could hardly bear watching him disappear in the sunny haze of the plains. She liked the man and his ability to play a part and then his bravery to admit it. Not everyone was cut out for violence, and face it, that's what this bunch was headed for. Pure and simple, someone might get killed. Whit chose to be useful in the only way he could.

Rose turned and climbed on Cimarron. She sure wished they knew what had happened to the man and who had done that to him. But they probably never would. Taking up the reins of the black, she led him off to the head of the line, wondering what would happen next to hold them up from reaching the Buckle D and confrontation with Amos Horner and Rafe Malone.

It wasn't long before she found out.

Not even half an hour later, ahead of the line she was first to spot a huge boiling cloud of dust off in the same direction. Seemed like you could ride this wide country for hours and appear not to get anywhere. She wished they were anywhere but here, even at the Buckle D engaged in a gunfight to stop Horner and Malone.

"What is that?" She reined in and pointed. "Looks like a stampede."

One by one, the riders following her drew to a halt, with Dell shouting at them not to bunch up.

In a very few minutes the ground began to tremble, the bay danced beneath her and the black, who'd had enough excitement for one day, reared on its hind legs and screamed. By the time she had him settled down the riders came in sight, at least the leading ones, who then reined in their mounts one-by-one. The dust cloud hovered, passed over them and drifted off into the air.

Must not have rained this far north. She lifted her bandana and wiped the grit from her eyes. There must've been fifteen or twenty riders, the first four or five approached their line, showing confusion over who to speak to. Dell settled it for them by riding to meet them. A bit nervous, Rose kept an eagle eye on them.

"I'm thinking on moving off." Jake had ridden up on her, so that she jerked around, startling Cimarron into a stiff legged buck.

She settled the Andalusian and snubbed in the nervous black who threatened to bolt. "Don't blame you, it looks like a posse. Wonder who they're after."

Jake spat. "In Texas? State ain't short of wanted outlaws, including me."

She couldn't help laughing. The entire situation was ridiculous. The panhandle was big enough on its own to have allowed the recent excitement to go on out of sight of their small bunch. It was almost as if something was working against them. What were they talking so long about? Were those riders perhaps on the trail of Rafe Malone, who had escaped prison or were they out hunting the arsonist just like Dell and them? Or like Jake said, one of many others.

Before Dell returned, the sound of an approaching rider dragged her attention in the opposite direction. There came Gil, riding fast. He'd made good time, and she hoped the news he carried from the fire wouldn't be terrible. This day was beginning to turn really sour on them. He drew up short of a gallop and walked his mount on in. Halted next to her.

"What did you learn?"

"What's going on here?" Both questions asked by each of them.

"You go first."

Keeping an eye on the other riders, Gil nodded. "Okay. It was a barn fire at a farm down toward Carlton. No one was hurt. They lost a couple of mules they used to plow with, which was bad enough, but not what it could've been, considering who's on the loose. They never seen anyone. Now you."

She grimaced. "Sorry, we really don't know. They just showed up like a stampede. We'll have to wait for Dell to tell us."

Gil surveyed the lineup. "Hey, where's our funny little friend and his little pinto pony?"

She filled him in on that excitement, and about the time she finished Dell rode back, the huge posse stirred into motion and headed on across to the east.

"Hmm, I guess they aren't looking for the same people we are." Rose studied Dell, not sure what to expect when he came back from palavering with the cowboys.

From the expression on his face, it couldn't be real good, yet they had taken off without bothering their little group.

Before he reached the head of their line, he signaled the others to join him. Nodding a welcome to Gil, he waited 'til the Apache who had been tailing the group caught up.

"It's bad news, sorry to say. It seems a church and the millinery were burnt to the ground yesterday in Carlton while we were down at Palo Duro. That posse is on the way down there to find out who might've done it, but they've got their suspicions, considering what's been going on around here the past few weeks. I tell you, this has got to stop before that son-of-a-bitch burns down the entire panhandle of Texas. The Rangers have sent a troop out to meet them down there."

"Then they're thinking Horner is down there and not up at the Buckle D? He didn't take our bait?" Rose was devastated.

"I'm thinking we need to go to Thomas City, for that's probably where we can catch us this fire starter. They think he might be headed that way. Jake, if you'd rather not be around that many lawmen, maybe you ought to go back to your bunch."

Jake stared off at the disappearing posse. "I'd like to see those men caught, but you're right. Those ole boys yonder would just as soon hang me from the closest tree while they're at it. Maybe me and my bunch can nose around and find out more about Malone and Horner without riding with you."

Sick at heart, Rose told Jake goodbye, then turned to Dell. "I don't think those boys are gonna want a bounty hunter riding with them, either. I'm gonna head on up north and see what I can learn from this Dawson fella at the Buckle D. You never can tell. He might have some insight into what Horner will do next. He sure isn't gonna stay out in the open with half the panhandle chasing him."

She hated to tell the bunch goodbye. It'd been kinda fun riding with lawmen for a change, but hell, she was a bounty hunter through and through, and she'd have to go her own way and trust her own instincts.

"Care if I take the black? I'll see he gets a good home."

Dell nodded. "See you around, Rosie. You take good care of yourself."

She tipped her hat, reared the Andalusian. "I'll let you know if I round up those owl hoots and get me that bounty. I'll even buy you a drink over in Cactus Junction."

"I'll hold you to that." His words lifted with the wind at her back.

Riding the trail alone after being in such good company gave her an empty feeling. The silence, broken only by the screech of an occasional hawk sailing low to look for prey, gave her time to consider what she would do if she found Horner and Malone.

Hunger chased her down even as the sun climbed high in the brilliant blue sky. In her search for shade, she came upon a cluster of trees growing beside a small rivulet of flowing water. Cimarron stopped on his own, then the black, both lowered their noses into the pool formed at the egress of the underground stream. She swung clear and dropped to her knees beside them to share the cool liquid.

Her eyes caught sight of boots pointing at the sky. Wiping her mouth, she stepped across the spring and pulled back the limbs to reveal a man lying on his back, arms spread wide. Even in the shadows she recognized his face.

"Wade Guthrie? Wade, is it you?"

She shook his shoulder. His face was bruised, and he moaned with pain when she touched him. "You're hurt. I thought you were dead. Where have you been?"

She hurried back to the stream, wet her bandana and went to him to clean his face and inspect the damage.

His eyes fluttered open, and he batted them a few times. "Rosie? Where did you come from? Am I dreaming or dead? Oh, man, everything hurts."

"Can you sit up?" She draped his arm over her shoulder and tried to help him.

"Why don't I just lay here a while first?"

"Okay, do you want a drink or anything? I'm dying to know what happened to you. When I left, they said you'd been killed, and I saw you go down. That's when I quit outlawing and took up bounty hunting, trying to find the man who killed you."

He managed a grin. "And did you, my outlaw queen?"

"No, some ranger killed him down in Laredo a year or so later. Wade, it's so good to see you alive."

"And this isn't a dream?" He touched her face with the fingers of one hand. "You feel real."

"So, tell me about it."

"Some Indians found me. Tewa tribesmen over around Taos, New Mexico. By the time I had recovered, months had passed. I didn't remember much of what had happened."

"How did you get here?" She continued to clean the dirt from his face. The wounds were not deep. Looked as if someone had a fist fight with him, then left him here. She looked around but saw no evidence of a mount.

"Where's your horse?"

He struggled to sit up and she gave him a hand. "Don't see one, they must've taken it."

"Who, they?"

"I hate to tell you this, but you know those men you were talking about?"

"Amos Horner and Rafe Malone? Wade, why didn't you tell me?"

"I am telling you."

"How long you been riding with them? Have you helped them burn ranches? Please tell me you haven't."

"Well, I haven't. They showed up at the canyon a few days ago. I was there, hiding from some rangers who had been on my tail for weeks. When they said they were going northwest I asked if I could go with them. Honest, I had no idea they were burning ranches 'til you just now told me. I saw it as a way to get out of the state. Those Texas Rangers were driving me crazy. Always one or another tailing me."

"Is there a wanted out on you?"

He nodded, stared at the ground between his folded legs. "They did this to me. I argued with one of them and we had a fight. I never was real good at fisticuffs. You know that, Rose. All I want is to get out of Texas. I'm thinking of Colorado, up in the mountains. I can't outlaw anymore. I'm bone tired, and it ain't a career one can feel safe in for as long as I have." His grey eyes were soft and reflected her. "You gonna shoot me, Rose? You'd really shoot me?"

"I still can't believe that, of all the places in all of the panhandle, you and I end up here at the same time. And I'm not going to shoot you, Wade. You and I…well, we've done too much together for me to do that. Look, sweetheart, I've got an extra horse. That big black yonder. You take him and you ride on to Colorado. Kiss me goodbye before you go."

"Where you going, Rosie?"

"To the Buckle D. I hope that's where Horner is going next and I'm going to stop him, once and for all."

He flexed both fists and crawled to his feet. "Then that's where I'm going too. You don't think I'm gonna let you take on those two toughs on your own, do you?"

"What about Colorado?"

"Well, then, I can go there after we finish here. And you can come with me."

Well, she didn't know about that, but having someone as good with a gun as Wade Guthrie would help assure that they could bring down their quarry. No trouble at all.

FIFTEEN

DELL HELD UP HIS REMAINING men in sight of Thomas City late that day. No smoke, no evidence of an uproar of any kind. Everything appeared peaceful.

"Okay, let's go on in, get a good night's sleep, then plan what to do next. Hate like the devil to have taken our time coming back here, but sure relieved to be wrong about trouble here."

He, Gil, Dutch, Brand, and Angelo rode down the quiet street through the small town. A few people walked the boardwalks, though it was getting on to supper time. In front of the jail, they tied their mounts. His jailer, Guy, stood in the doorway.

"Didn't 'spect you back this soon. Did you miss him?"

"Tell you about it later." Dell crawled off his horse, trail weary, thirsty, and hungry. "One of you take the horses down to the livery and see they're properly cared for. If we're tired, they're wore out. And unload that pack horse, too, if you don't mind."

Gil volunteered, gathering the reins. The Apache remained mounted, watching them as if not sure what to do.

Gil paused. "Boss, you going back out after this outlaw, or what? If so,

I'd like to go along. Hate to start anything I don't finish. Besides, I'm still officially a deputy, ain't I?"

Dell paused on the steps to the sheriff's office. "Tell you what, Gil. You show up here first thing in the morning, ready to ride. I hate not to finish what I start as well. Those yahoos have had time to ride over here and wreak havoc. I'm thinking on swinging through Carlton in the morning. See what those marshals and that posse turned up. If nothing we're heading for the Buckle D to carry out our original plan. I still think it's a good idea."

Guinn was in the living room sewing a patch on a pair of his britches when he walked up to the door and burst through the screen. Eyes huge, she leaped from her chair dropping the mending.

"My goodness, you scared me half to death. Are you all right? What happened? Did you catch them? Where's Curly? That's why I didn't hear you."

He took her in his arms, dust puffing from his clothes and out of his hair. She kissed him and laughed. "You're gritty. There's water in the reservoir. I had a fire a while ago, so it's probably still hot. You can tell me while you bathe."

"After that hug, you might need a bath too. Sorry, I was just so glad to see you." He headed for the kitchen unbuttoning his shirt.

After a hot bath and some supper, he told her all that had happened, then broke the bad news.

"We're going back out in the morning. Sent Curly down to the livery so they could care for him. Whew, he's as wore out as I am. I'm so sorry to be leaving you again. Lord, I'll be glad when this is over. Going to see which way the marshals and posse went from Carlton, then if they ain't going in the direction of the Buckle D Ranch we'll ride on up there. We'll trap these two evil doers if we have to ride all over the state of Texas."

She took his face in both hands and kissed him. "Hmm, smell nice and clean. Just like a man I'd like to take to bed. I'll bet you're too tired to do anything, so we'll just hold each other."

He kissed her palm. "I'm never too tired to do anything with my lovely wife, Guinn."

"Oh, is that right? Well, let's just see, then."

He slept better that night than he had in a while, even worries about stopping the fire starter didn't keep him awake. The woman he loved gave him back all the love he needed.

The next morning, he repacked his bedroll, saddlebag and other gear. It looked like too much to pile on Curly, so he rode back down to the livery and arranged to rent the faithful pack horse they'd used before. When he came out of the livery leading the animal, Gil, Brand, and Dutch were waiting. Each man had a sack and rearranged it all as before.

"Well, fellas, looks like we're headed back to the Buckle D to finish what we started. I had Guy wire down to Carlton and heard back that the rangers, some marshals and deputies spread out all over the southwest to find and catch the fire starter. They think he took out for New Mexico. We may prove them wrong. If we don't, then we'll have had a nice ride."

"We going back to the northwest, Boss?" Gil looked eager to light out, dancing his horse in his anxiety to get going.

"Yep, I got a feeling in my bones, and my bones ain't very often wrong. We ain't careful, Horner'll set fire to the whole panhandle."

Everyone packed up and ready, Dell led them out of town. Not a mile later, a rider approached from off to the left. They slowed and Antonio fell in line with them. Dell was glad to see the Apache.

By noon they had left the main trail and cut across the plains toward the Buckle D Ranch. The grasses of spring swished around Curly's galloping hooves. It was such a purty day, Dell held back the curses that struggled to spout from his tongue.

He was so danged mad at himself for turning back the day before, but he needed to slow down. No man is any good out here without his horse and riding one to death was one of the worst sins. Besides, they'd need water soon. There was a dry weather spring not too far on down the trail, if that posse hadn't drunk it dry yesterday, which would mean waiting 'til it filled back up. Behind him, the hoof beats of his men's animals pounded the earth. Maybe they'd catch up with Rosie if they pushed on, but she was on that long-legged bay that could run all day and into the night, so it wasn't likely. It would be a bad deal if she took on those two ruffians all alone.

Shortly, Curly caught scent of the water and wanted to go, so he let him. It wasn't far and they could all rest there in the shade where a few trees grew in the moist soil.

Two horses were tied to a line on the far side of the spring. He halted, held up a hand to signal the others behind him and stood in his stirrups. The familiar red bay with his eight black points stood beside a black he'd seen before.

Rosie.

Thank God she had decided to wait for him to return from Thomas City.

"Let's go, boys. It's Rosie. Hope she left some water for us."

There was no sign of anyone at the spring. Dang, what was going on? Had someone ambushed her? Not possible, or they'd have taken the horses. He signaled the men to stay mounted and slowly stepped down. Dropping the reins, he walked soundlessly to the spring, then headed for the trees, pulling his .45 and holding it down by his side. Someone was over there talking and laughing. Stepping into the shade, he halted.

"Step out into the open and drop your gun." A woman's voice. Rosie.

"Rosie, it's me, Dell Hoffman. You talking to yourself?"

Laughing, she emerged from the woods, a man following her. Who in thunder was that? He looked vaguely familiar. He never forgot a face, especially if it were on someone he'd arrested. The gun he'd holstered came out again.

"Wade Guthrie? Rosie, do you know who that is?"

"Put your gun away, Sheriff. He's on our side. Going to ride with us to take care of the fire starter and that dreadful Rafe Malone."

"He's a scoundrel, Rose. Do you know that?"

Both of them laughed. "Oh, she knows it, Sheriff Hoffman, but I don't turn on my friends, and Rosie is a friend. You could be, too, or at least temporarily while we hunt down these killers. Then, if you like, I could go back to my scoundrel ways, and you could chase me all over Texas just for fun."

"He means it, Dell." Her calling him Dell reminded him they were friends, and he could trust her judgment.

"All right, just for this once. I'm not in the habit of riding with outlaws but looks like this here trip is changing that daily. I'll take all the help I can get to run down these particular ones."

"Does that mean I can come out now?" Wade stepped from behind Rose. "Good to see you again, Sheriff."

"Uh-huh, we'll see. Just remember, I've got my eye on you. You point that six-shooter any way but at these two outlaws we're chasing, I'll come down on you."

Wade held up his hands in surrender. "I hear you, Sheriff. I hear you."

Rosie walked back toward the others, Wade behind her. "I take it all is well in Thomas City."

"Yes. I'm surprised to find you still here. Figured by now you'd be over there at the Buckle D setting up an ambush for your favorite outlaw."

She glanced up at Wade, and he grinned down at her. Ah, besotted, they were. "Never mind, I don't need any explanations." He turned to the men still mounted. "Well, come on. We stopped for water and a bit of a rest for the animals. Let's get it done so we can move on. I'd like to be there before dark if we can. The head start they've got, it wouldn't surprise me if they don't attack late tonight or early next morning. We need to be ready."

"YOU'RE ABSOLUTELY SURE RAFE AND Amos will be at the Buckle D." Rose addressed Dell while she helped fill canteens from the mouth of the spring and the horses drank in the pool formed below.

Her favorite sheriff appeared a bit miffed by her friendship with Wade. Maybe he sensed it was more than a friendship, but it didn't matter, since her personal life was none of his business. She capped the canteen, handed it to Brand and reached out for another. The stranger named Gil handed one over and she filled it.

"Glad to see you returned with the sheriff. He says you're a crack shot."

"I'm pleased to be invited for this roundup, especially with such famous folks. I've heard plenty about both you and Wade Guthrie."

"Well, it's foolish to believe everything you hear about anyone."

He took the filled canteen from her. "I'll try to remember that. Anyway, it's my pleasure to ride with you."

She smiled at him. What a strange-spoken man for a farmer in the wilds of the Texas panhandle. All kinds were moving out here. One day there'd probably be cities the size of Amarillo up here. And people like her and Wade and even Sheriff Hoffman would no longer ride these wide-open plains. She shook her head and put her mind elsewhere. Mostly to gunning down Rafe and Amos both, which she intended to do if she got the chance.

Sheriff Hoffman climbed on his horse. "Time to head out. Rosie, would you and Wade bring up the rear and make sure we aren't set upon by any other outlaws."

Rose couldn't resist. "I notice we're missing Jake Harper. Isn't he going with us this time?"

Dell gave her a long look, like maybe she ought to watch her mouth. She laughed and swung onto her bay. The Andalusian performed a circle, then waited to fall in beside Wade's big black. The others strung out ahead of them and set a decent pace that would put the miles behind them on the flat plains.

The day grew hotter as the sun climbed overhead. Spring was definitely turning into summer. If it weren't for the breeze that seldom ever quit blowing on the plains everyone would be downright miserable. Rose glanced at Wade and found him looking at her. How strange, as big as the west was, that he and she should come together at a deserted spring. One might almost believe in fate, or lightning striking twice, if one believed in anything like that at all.

"What you thinking, Rosie?"

"Oh, nothing much. About lightning striking, about wishes and dreams."

"Mmm. You ever think of the old days at Dottie Lou's?"

"Not if I can help it. That wasn't me, you know. It was a different person— a woman caught in a trap of sorts."

"How is your mama these days?" His expression told her he understood the trap.

"She's dead, Wade. Oh, I'm not all broken up or anything. I'm sorry, but you know how it was between us. She held me captive 'til I was old enough to break free. So, there's no love lost between us. Still, I hate that she died the way she did. Burned up in that cabin by that maniac. No one deserves that."

"Oh, Rose, I'm sorry, I hadn't heard. I've been over in New Mexico, a hired gun for the range wars. Got tired of the politicking."

"That must've been exciting."

"Well, not exactly."

The Apache reined in quickly. Ahead, Dell had called a halt. He signaled them to stay there, and he took off riding fast and low in the saddle. The cap rock had been dropping off for the past hour or more so that the land lay exposed far below them. And down there, looking much like a toy was spread a vast ranch. Dell must think it was the Buckle D and was going to check it out.

Reluctant to let him go alone, just in case his idea of an ambush backfired on him, she kicked Cimarron into a full out gallop and went after him. He hauled up a way ahead of her. She said nothing when she caught up. Just waited for him to speak.

"Reckon that's it?"

"Best way to find out is ride on in, slow and non-threatening. Two people all alone."

He looked her up and down. "You ever pay any attention to what you're told?"

"About like you do, Sheriff. Shall we go on down? Meet the owner of the Buckle D. He might as well know what we're up to. Every one of us rides in, he's liable to take some pot shots at us." She glanced at him. "Unless you've got a better idea."

He chuckled. "I thought I did, but mine ain't as good. I was gonna sneak up on 'em and jump out and scare 'em."

"I don't believe that."

"Wise woman. Come on, let's go check this place out. We might be riding into an ambush ourselves, so be on your toes."

A woman met them out in the yard, a rifle in one hand, the other shading her eyes from the sun to see better. Obviously, they didn't look too threatening, she let them advance and get down off the horses.

Rose stepped forward. "Hello, ma'am. Is this the Buckle D Ranch?"

"It is. What do you want?"

Rose looked at Dell. Time he said something. "I'm Sheriff Dell Hoffman of Thomas City. I have to talk to you and your husband about something. Is he here?"

"Not at the present, but some of his men are within hailing distance in case you have any ideas."

"I'm sorry, ma'am, that we frightened you. We're pursuing a couple of really dangerous outlaws. You wouldn't happened to have seen them?"

She blanched. "Lord no. All we ever see out here are cattle, chickens, horses, and an occasional bird flies over. You can come on in out of this sun. It's mighty hot today. I have fresh lemonade but no ice."

"That would be wonderful. Rose, why don't you go inside with Missus—uh?"

"King, Loretta King."

"Missus King. We have several men with us, as you might understand, and I'd like to go tell them it's all right to come on in, perhaps water their horses at your tank yonder and themselves at your pump, if that's okay, too."

Rose laughed to herself at the woman's expression. Something was happening she wasn't sure she wanted, but she had no idea how to put a stop to it. Or if she should try. She'd seen the expression before. Missus King wanted Mister King. Now.

"I'll send one of the men to get my husband, if you don't mind."

Rose spoke up. "Perhaps we could wait to get the men until your husband comes."

"Oh, well. Oh, no, it's all right to go get them now. He will be right here."

Dell climbed back up on his horse and heeled him into a run.

Missus King watched for a minute, then came back to herself and escorted Rose inside. It was cool in the house, all the windows open and the curtains dancing in the afternoon breeze.

The floors were shiny, the rooms immaculate. If they'd already had male visitors of the outlaw kind the place wouldn't look like this. Missus King led her into the kitchen, seated her at a square table and poured her a glass of lemonade. Sunlight through the window sparkled in the yellow drink.

"Thank you." Instead of raising the glass, Rose peered out the kitchen window. A shadow moved out there, close to the ground. Perhaps a dog, but she palmed her Colt, anyway.

The woman stepped between her and the view. Everything happened at once. The screen door slammed open. A man launched himself through it. Rose slapped at her gun and dropped to the floor. The lemonade spilled out across the table. The Colt skidded out of her reach. A hand clamped around her arm. Yanked her to her feet. She came face to face with the man she'd done her best to kill five years ago.

Rafe Malone's frightening grimace revealed green teeth and breathed stinking air all over her. Repulsed she gagged, clawed at him with a free hand and did her best to kick as he brought her upright.

In the background a wrenching scream from Missus King.

"Shut her up," Malone demanded and the other man who'd followed him in hit the woman with his fist, knocking her up against the cookstove. The scream was cut off and she melted to the floor like molasses.

The man turned to Malone. "Is this the one you wanted?"

"This is her. What do we do now?" Malone twisted her arm to the middle of her back and with his crippled hand stuffed his bandana in her mouth.

"Wait for the husband and kids. I want them all here for the big show."

Kids? Oh, no. Good they didn't know Dell and his men were out there. This bunch came in from the back. Must've spotted her through the kitchen window and thought she had come alone. Dell would ride in soon and if they came right up in the yard these two would pick them off before they knew what had happened.

Dell had asked for the men to take their horses to the tank out in the pasture to drink. If they did that it would give her a chance to warn them somehow before they rode into a trap. But how?

THE MEN GATHERED ANXIOUSLY AROUND Dell, Brand speaking first. "Boss, everything okay down there? Is this the right ranch?"

He wished he knew. Despite or because of the woman's reaction to their arrival, he got that feeling up and down his spine. Like a lizard played there. It wasn't anything new. Something was amiss, but he didn't know what. He just felt they ought to proceed with caution instead of riding in like a parade or something.

"Tell you what …." He stopped 'cause someone was missing, and he'd almost forgot about him. "Where's that Wade fellow?"

They all looked around. None knew, no one had seen him leave. "Reckon he decided to light out, didn't want no part of this?"

Some of them nodded. Angelo interrupted their muttered suppositions.

"He go." The Apache pointed off down the hill toward the ranch.

"You saw him? Did he tell you anything?"

The silent man shook his head, spread a hand over his chest. "I will go? Fetch?"

"No, that's okay. Stay here with us." Dell dismounted. "I've got an idea, just in case this lizard is right."

"Lizard, Boss?" the men asked, looking at him as if he were crazy.

"We're gonna tie the horses to those bushes over there and walk down, or rather sneak down to see what's up. I want you to fan out in a circle up here where likely they won't notice. It's a ways down there. Seek cover where you can and stay low. I'll go to the far side of the house, and when I get in place I'll whistle like a hawk's cry, then give you a few minutes. When I whistle again, we'll all start toward the house, still seeking cover. When I whistle the third time, be ready to go in guns pulled. But remember, there are two women in there, be careful who you shoot. Okay?" He gazed at Angelo. *"Entiende?"*

The Apache nodded and took off moving low and fast to a copse nearby.

Gil chuckled. "I'm pretty sure he got the first part, now if he doesn't bust in down there and scalp 'em all 'fore we can stop him."

Gil had become more at home with the group. Maybe he'd see about pinning a badge on him permanently if this went like he hoped. Brand and Dutch got along with him, and the way the town was growing ...well, this wasn't the time, but he'd think about it.

He sent each man one by one to surround the ranch house. He took the farthest spot, so they'd all be ready to go when he signaled. Hunching along from one bush, rock and tree to the next took forever. He hoped none of the men grew restless and imagined, or a hawk happened to fly over and give that screeching whistle they made when hunting prey.

He finally drew up opposite of where he'd begun. The other men must be in place. He whistled, waited counting to sixty three times, then whistled again. Hopefully each man was now approaching the house. A third whistle would tell them to bust in, guns drawn and shoot anything that wasn't a woman, a child or an old person. He gave them time, was proud that he couldn't see any of them work their way to the house, hoped they were actually there.

He put his hand on the back screen-door handle and whistled. All hell broke loose. Men shouted, guns went off and women screamed. The sound of guns going off inside the house was deafening. Inside he couldn't hear much of anything and the smoke made it hard to see. A man tried to dart past him, and he grabbed hold, getting a look at his face.

"Who are you, what's your name?" He shook him hard.

"King. My name's King. What's going on here?"

"Mister King, I'm Sheriff Hoffman from Thomas City, here to arrest Rafe Malone and Amos Horner. Try to find your wife and take her into the bedroom. She'll be safe there. You have children?"

"They're down in the cellar. I sent' em there when I expected something was wrong."

"Go, get your wife. Rose, you here?"

"Boss, I got this 'un swears he's a hired hand."

"Take him to the bedroom. Mister King should be there with his wife. He can tell you. He don't look like anyone I know, but I never saw Amos in the flesh, though I do know Malone. Dammit, let's find the two of them. Can't let 'em get away."

Hard to see a blamed thing in all the gunsmoke. How in thunder were they gonna lay hands on those two in this?

SIXTEEN

GUNSMOKE HUNG IN THE SUDDEN stillness of the Buckle D ranch house. From the distance thunder rumbled as if trying to outdo the blast of the gunfight. Dell hollered for everyone to join him. Counting heads left both Wade and Antonio missing. Danged if he could take the time to look for them. They'd have to make it on their own and he'd have to hope he could count on them. Wonder what Amos did with his kid? Probably got shed of him one way or the other.

Thunder rumbled and lightning flashed, not helping one bit in the gloom of the room. He dared not make another sound 'til he could place everyone and knew they could do the same. Not good to have one of his men shoot another.

The bedroom door creaked open, and King and his wife crept out. Dell grabbed them. Everyone huddled close to the floor, gazing at him.

"Where'd they go, boss?"

Dell hissed at Gil to be still. Turned to King. "How do we get the kids out of the cellar?"

King pointed to the floor in one corner. "There's a door there, prize it up. A tool is under the wash basin."

"Dear God. We have to get them out of there, and now. Amos will try to burn us out. Where's your barn from here? Yonder, isn't it?" Dell pointed in the opposite direction from where the outlaws had fired on them. That they had stopped could only mean they were planning something.

King nodded. "Yes, it's there."

"Okay, get that cellar door open now and—" A shot broke the back kitchen window and slammed into the opposite wall. Another followed through the side window breaking a lamp on the cupboard. Glass flew in all directions.

His biggest problem was getting those kids out of the cellar. Dealing with a fire starter could get them trapped down there. And worse, these dry timber houses could go up in flames fast. He had to do something to keep Amos from setting the house ablaze. He probably carried the stuff to do it in his saddlebags. Their horses were bound to be close by.

"We've got to work fast. If Horner sets this house afire, we might not get out. Or if we did, we could get shot down. We'll go out in the direction of the barn, the house between us and them. But we gotta get those girls up here first."

"Don't waste your bullets. Don't fire unless you can see the shooters. Go on, stay low and get that cellar door open. Soon as he brings the kids up get to those windows and lay down cover fire." He pointed at the Kings. "When we start firing you two take your kids out the front door and into the barn. And listen, do me a favor. Go straight to Carlton or on to Cactus Junction. Find a ranger or a marshal and tell them what's going on up here. Give them the names of your posse that burned this maniac out. In case he gets away he's gonna burn them out. Got that?"

The Kings nodded. "You got horses in there, mount up and ride off as fast as you can. Keep the house between you and them. Don't bother with saddles just get on their backs and ride. Ride hard and fast, don't worry about us. We'll keep 'em busy back here. Help can never arrive in time. We'll settle this, once and for all. Now get moving."

The storm moved closer, the rumble becoming blasts. Lightning that had lit the sky now appeared to slam to earth in long bony fingers, visible through the broken windows. Rain turned loose then, the noise on the roof like a huge waterfall.

Several large tree trunks in the back yard offered good shelter for Amos and Rafe to hide behind, but Dell and his crew could lay down fire to keep them from shooting at the family until they ran out of bullets. Then what? He'd figure that out when it happened.

One big thing was on Dell's and his men's side. The furious rain would put out any fire Amos tried to set. But he wouldn't leave. Not 'til he accomplished what he came here for. Rafe was no doubt the same. Men like these rarely gave up, so that left only one course of action. Stop them the only way possible. Dell had no doubt this would end right here, because he was not letting them go out there and wreak more havoc on the people he protected. So, it would be a fight to the bitter end.

King came up the ladder out of the cellar carrying two girls.

"Down, get down. Crawl to the door." Their crying nearly broke Dell's heart. He fanned a hand in gesture. He'd see they got out if he had to die trying. King handed the smallest to his wife. Without saying anything they cradled the girls, now screaming with terror, and crawled on the floor to the front door.

Beyond fear, Dell nodded, reloaded and joined Rose, Brand, Dutch, and Gil in laying down fire so the Kings could get out of the house and to the barn. Return shots continued to cut chunks from the walls and rain debris down on them. A strange silence followed the King family leaving the house, as if the crying of the girls had caused a peace, of sorts, in spite of the gunfire. The pounding of hoof beats said the family was away.

Damn if they were hitting anyone, just laying down fire toward the trees from where the shots were coming. In the bright flashes he caught shadows of their quick movement. Dell reloaded from his belt and told the others to do the same. They'd given the family all the time they could.

From outside bullets continued to chink through windows and into the kitchen, breaking dishes and tearing chunks out of the walls. Dell signaled his bunch to stop firing and they did. Once the two men outside realized it, they stopped firing too.

He peered through the lower part of a broken window. Dammit, they had their horses. Were they trying to get away? The rain hid so much of what was going on. Maybe they planned on riding up and through the doors, firing on everyone. On the other hand, he had them outnumbered, maybe they were leaving.

At any minute, the two might rush the house from a different direction. Nothing more had been seen of them, just that constant attack without pause.

Now, silence.

Were they out of ammo? Were they sneaking up on the house, maybe to set it afire?

A bolt of lightning struck a huge tree, splitting it open and sending half to the ground. In the light created he squinted to see them hunched low. And something else. Two men riding through trees behind them. Could it be Antonio and Wade? He didn't have long to wait. They cut loose on the two behind the burning tree. Those two split up and took off, hunkered low.

He hand-signaled each of his bunch to cover a side window where they could take a chance to peer out, try to pinpoint where the two outlaws had gone. Where in the hell was Antonio? About then another rider, huge in the saddle, passed the light and disappeared. He had help outside.

"Take care Don't show yourselves. Wade and Antonio are out there. Don't make targets out of them."

All five watched and waited. There was a pause in the storm, as if it was getting ready to attack as well. It was so quiet he could hear them breathing. His ears rang from all the gunfire in the enclosed space. Any minute now, something would happen. If Amos used dynamite, he might succeed in his desire to burn the place. Worse was they couldn't see either of the outlaws. Maybe best if they made a run for it, laying down fire. The three in the woods could do the same when they saw what was happening. At least they had saved the family.

A blood-curdling scream cut the air, as if the hordes of hell had been released. An Indian war whoop and a volley of shots sounded from beyond the two outlaws. Three horsemen rode in from that direction. Pistols smoking, they drove the two out of hiding. And that Indian probably scared them right out of their britches with that war whoop.

"Stop him. He's going around the house." Someone yelled from the back yard.

Rose shouted. "That's Wade! Antonio's with him."

Dell charged out on the front porch.

A man on horseback rode around the corner laying down fire. Antonio pursued him, let go an arrow and it thunked into its target. The sky went white, lit Amos Horner with an arrow in his arm, his face tortured. He lifted his gun, saw Dell, whirled and took a shot that clipped his ear.

Hot blood ran through his shirt onto his shoulder. Damn, that hurt more than he'd thought it would. Instead of firing again, Horner howled, threw down his gun, hugged his mount's neck and rode out across the barnyard. The horse lurched up a rise, through the mud and out of sight in the rain.

Uncertain as to where Rafe was, Dell swung around just as Rose jumped off the porch, aimed at something he couldn't see and fired. She ran forward and fired again, this time emptying her gun. Her target cried out in pain and then was quiet. She disappeared and Dell whirled to see if Amos had escaped or was coming back. By then the others had joined him on the porch.

"Should we go after him, Boss?" Gil peered through the waterfall pouring off the roof.

Dell stared for a moment, not sure what to do. A fierce streak of lightning jagged its way from high in the sky, splitting a tumbling ashen cloud and striking its target perfectly.

The man and horse waited on the rise, the mount reaching for the sky in a powerful rear, as if fighting back against the vicious finger of God that struck them square, exploding sparks in every direction like a fireworks display. Man and horse dropped, the rain moved on, the storm stilled. Perhaps it had done its job.

Breathing heavily, Dell leaned against the porch post. Then he stared up into a clearing sky. "Justice was done. Nothing like lightning in Texas. Sometimes it appears to reach up from the ground plumb into infinity." He smiled. "Is everyone okay?"

"Do you believe that, Boss?" Gil asked in a husky voice.

"Not yet, but I reckon I'll come to."

The remainder of his odd posse stared at the empty rise as if hypnotized. Jake rode in a circle, then dismounted. Wade soon joined them and jumped down to greet everyone. "I was afraid I'd be too late for the party. Just did make it. Sorry I didn't get here sooner."

"You all did exceptional today. I was worried for a while. Looks like Rose and Wade will have a hefty reward to share. Jake, I'm not sure how this comes out for you. Last I knew outlaws couldn't collect rewards on other outlaws."

"Or wouldn't want to," Jake added.

"Well, hell, I guess that leaves me out, too." Wade yanked off his wet hat.

Rose scuffed a boot in the wet grass. "I might be willing to give you a share if you hadn't come so late to the party. And you too, Jake, maybe it won't be much."

Everyone laughed, Jake punched Wade on the shoulder. "Maybe we earned enough to have some beers in Cactus Junction."

"I'll leave the three of you to divvy it up any way you see fit. Just don't kill each other over it," Dell said.

Their mood being what it was, this brought on another round of laughter.

When he could, Dell went on. "Officers of the law are not allowed to collect rewards. This I know. Gil, that'll hold for you, too, I'm sorry to say. I swore you in, so you're a deputy."

Gil shrugged. "That's okay, Sheriff. I'm just grateful to be alive. That was pretty exciting"

"Looks like no one was hurt."

Brand gestured toward Dell. "Yeah, what's that running out of your ear?"

Dell chuckled. "What's this? This isn't even a flesh wound. I was thinking of having a hole poked there anyway, you know like Antonio has. Put a fancy doo-dad in it."

For a moment there was total silence, then Antonio came from behind the house. Everyone laughed, then laughed some more. He looked all around, from one face to the other. Broke into a broad grin. "Got them, then."

TO ROSE IT WAS A relief to be done with this business. She had never gone after outlaws with a group of men. Sure made her nervous, not quite knowing what they'd do or how they'd act. It hadn't been too bad, but she preferred a lone hunt and catch. Dell more or less took charge, but that was okay, she trusted him. Just like he was doing now.

"Rose, you and Wade might want to gather up Horner's and Malone's bodies. If you can catch Malone's horse, I think it should go to Rose. She put him down. Besides she needs him to haul in her proof of death on both men. Did anyone see if Horner's horse lived through that lightning strike?"

No one had so Wade volunteered. "We'll check when we get the body."

"We don't usually bother with hauling the entire bodies in anymore, Dell." Rose put her elbow in Wade's side and grinned.

Dell held up both hands. "Wait one minute. I'm not sure I want to hear the answer to my question, but I'll ask it, anyway. Are we talking chopping off heads here?"

"You tell him, Wade." She still couldn't bring herself to come out with it.

Wade shuddered. "I can't, 'cause I'm afraid one of these days it'll be my head in that tow sack. I don't even want to think about it."

Jake put in his two cents worth. "You're afraid? I'm okay with it, just so long as it isn't Rose who collects on my head."

"Aw, now, Rosie, how does a delicate girl like you manage such as that?" Dell's eyes twinkled.

"I don't think you want to know that either. First off, admit I'm not a delicate girl."

Everyone in the yard burst out laughing, Brand and Gil exchanging blows on their shoulders and bounced around on the balls of their feet. It was the way men always released the fear they couldn't admit to in front of anyone. Laughed it off.

Rose sometimes wished women had the same ability. Women, they always tucked away bad experiences, and saved them for a rainy day. A day when nothing went well, and they brought out all their fears and lost expectations in one big burst of tears.

"I think the best thing for us to do now is run down the King family, though they don't have much of a home to return to. Haul these two bodies away from here where the proper—uh—*arrangements* can be made, then head for home." She sent Wade a look only he might understand. That they needed to get together somewhere for a few days.

Dell agreed. "Guinn will be happy to see me, and I hope to stay home for at least a month before I even leave town for anything."

"I'll be happy to start my job soon as we get back. I can handle my farm on my days off." Gil looked satisfied to be starting in as a deputy soon.

Brand and Dutch both enjoyed that by teasing him. "That's what all we deputies do, 'cause the pay isn't enough to live on."

"Say, I wonder what ole Whit did, how he got along taking that body in. He told me he was from back East and never rode a horse 'til he came out here, and he thought it would be exciting to be a cowboy." Rose helped drag Rafe's body out back to where his horse was tied. "Said that was why he rode that little pony, so if he got bucked off, he wouldn't have so far to fall."

"You must be joking." Dell had a look of disbelief on his face. "I never knew that. I wondered why he walked all over town and hardly ever rode that pony. How'd he get hired as town marshal? Wish I'd gone to that town council meeting. Usually, I never sat in on one— made excuses to be real busy with something else. What did he tell 'em, you reckon? 'Hey, I always wanted to be a cowboy'?"

He looked around. "Where's that Antonio? I want to thank him, too. He was just purely here 'cause I talked Julio into lending him to me for this little fandango. He was gonna do our tracking. Instead, we needed him for something else entirely."

Rose covered her mouth. "All this time and I forgot to tell him that one of the horseshoes on Horner's horse had a strange jagged lightning strike crack through it."

Everyone stopped what they were doing and stared at Rose. "What?" she said, then it hit her. She held a hand over her mouth.

Wade's eyes grew wide. "A lightning strike. Now, ain't that just about the strangest thing you ever heard?"

"If I believed in fate, I'd say it was telling me something with that shoe. But I guess I don't. All the same...." Rose shivered.

Dell helped her boost the limp body across the horse's back. "Well, there's nothing like lightning in Texas, I don't reckon."

Wade and Jake lifted the dead fire starter onto a horse. "Better tie their feet to their arms so they don't fall off."

"Wait," Brand hollered, running to catch up. "I want to see Rose chop that ole boy's head off and put it in a tow sack."

"Another time, Brand," she shouted back. "The hard work's done now."

"Well, it was a good day's work. Reckon we can start back home. Wonder if we can find the King family. They're probably still running." Dell stared out across the pasture in the direction the family had gone. "I reckon they'll stop when they get to town. That's what I'm gonna do. Stop in Thomas City where my purty wife is waiting. Let's get moving."

DUSTY RICHARDS GREW UP RIDING horses and watching his western heroes on the big screen. He even wrote book reports for his classmates, making up westerns since English teachers didn't read that kind of book. His mother didn't want him to be a cowboy, so he went to college, then worked for Tyson Foods and auctioned cattle when he wasn't an anchor on television.

His lifelong dream, though, was to write the novels he loved. He sat on the stoop of Zane Grey's cabin and promised he'd one day get published, as well. In 1992, that promise became a reality when his first book, *Noble's Way,* hit the shelves. In the years since, he published over 160 more, winning nearly every major award for western literature along the way. His 150th novel, *The Mustanger and the Lady,* was adapted for the silver screen and released as the motion picture *Painted Woman* in 2017. In a review for the movie, *True West* magazine proclaimed Dusty "the greatest living western fiction writer alive."

Sadly, Dusty passed away in early 2018, leaving behind a legion of fans and a legacy of great western writing that will live on for generations.

Facebook: westernauthordustyrichards
www.dustyrichards.com

www.ingramcontent.com/pod-product-compliance
Lightning Source LLC
Chambersburg PA
CBHW032005240626
47153CB00003B/1125